ELIZABETH VON ARNIM

(1866–1941) was born Mary Annette Beauchamp in Sydney, Australia, and brought up in England. Travelling in Italy with her father in 1889, she met her first husband, Count Henning August von Arnim-Schlagenthin. They were married in London the following year and lived in Berlin. After five years of marriage the von Arnims moved to their family estate, Nassenheide, in Pomerania: Elizabeth's experience and deep love of Nassenheide were to be wittily encapsulated in her first and most famous novel, *Elizabeth and Her German Garden*, published anonymously in 1898. The twenty-one books she then went on to write were signed 'By the author of Elizabeth and Her German Garden', and later simply 'By Elizabeth'.

Elizabeth von Arnim gave birth to four daughters and a son, whose tutors at Nassenheide included E. M. Forster and Hugh Walpole. Her idyllic Prussian days were, however, to be abruptly ended when, in 1908, debt forced the von Arnims to sell the estate. They moved to England, and in 1910 Count von Arnim died. Buying a site in Switzerland, Elizabeth built the Château Soleil where she worked on her books and entertained such friends as H. G. Wells (with whom she had an affair), Katherine Mansfield (her cousin), John Middleton Murry and Frank Swinnerton. On the outbreak of war she managed to escape to England, but she was unable to rescue her daughter Felicitas, who died in Germany. In 1916 Elizabeth von Arnim married Francis, second Earl Russell, brother of Bertrand Russell, whom she had met three years previously. This proved to be a disastrous union: in the first year of marriage Elizabeth ran away to America, and in 1919 the couple finally separated.

A greatly admired literary figure of her time, described by Alice Meynell as 'one of the three finest wits of her day', Elizabeth spent her later years in Switzerland, London, and the French Riviera where she wrote her autobiography, *All the Dogs of My Life* (1936). On the outbreak of the Second World War she moved to America, where she died two years later at the age of seventy-five.

Of her novels Virago publishes *Vera, Fräulein Schmidt and Mr Anstruther, Elizabeth and Her German Garden, The Enchanted April, The Pastor's Wife, Love, The Caravaners, The Adventures of Elizabeth in Rügen* and *The Solitary Summer*.

VIRAGO
MODERN
CLASSIC

NUMBER

382

Elizabeth von Arnim

THE
SOLITARY
SUMMER

Nature nous a estrenez d'une large faculté à nous entretenir à part; et nous y appelle souvent, pour nous apprendre que nous nous debvons en partie à la societé, mais en la meilleure partie à nous.
MONTAIGNE, *Essais*, ii. 18.

Published by VIRAGO PRESS Limited 1993
20–23 Mandela Street, Camden Town, London NW1 OHQ

First published in Great Britain by Macmillan & Co. 1899

Introduction Copyright © Deborah Kellaway 1993

A CIP catalogue record for this book is available from the British Library

Printed and bound in Great Britain by
Cox & Wyman Ltd, Reading, Berks.

TO

THE MAN OF WRATH

WITH

SOME APOLOGIES

AND

MUCH LOVE

INTRODUCTION

On a late afternoon in May 1897, a young woman sat outside in the warm fresh air after a shower of rain and wrote: "I love my garden." It was the first sentence of an anonymous work which became a best-seller, running into twenty-one reprints in its first twelve months, and thereafter regularly reprinting several times a year until 1914. When Macmillan accepted the manuscript, it was the most "purely happy moment" of the young author's life, too happy to be described, so she simply noted in her journal: "Got answer re G. G. accepting it." "G.G." was shorthand for *Elizabeth and Her German Garden*, the inspired title of a book that was less about a garden than about its vivacious author's responses to her life. No sooner had she corrected its proofs than she embarked on its sequel: *The Solitary Summer*. She began it in July 1898, finished seven months later, and Macmillan brought it out in 1899 to a chorus of critical acclaim: "In many respects a great advance" — *Country Gentleman* ... "Herein is ripeness that was missing from the earlier book" — *London Letter* ... "An author who can endow all she touches with life" — *Manchester Guardian*. It was again anonymous. The title page simply said: "By the author of *Elizabeth and Her German Garden*".

So who was she? Speculation as to her identity can only have added to the allure of the books. She presented herself as German, but her English was faultlessly idiomatic, though the noted man of letters, Arthur Quiller-Couch, pointed out (much to her chagrin) that she split the occasional infinitive. Was she really English? Was she a daughter of Queen Victoria? Was she a woman at all? Might she be the poet laureate, Alfred Austin, who had already written a book in discursive, journal form called *The Garden that I Love*? Or was she the young English wife of the Count von Arnim?

The last guess was the right one. She was indeed the Countess von Arnim, and her "garden" was the park of a vast estate in Pomerania. But she was not German and her name was not "Elizabeth". Her maiden name was Mary Annette Beauchamp; she was born in New Zealand in 1866. The first three years of her life were spent in a fine house overlooking Sydney Harbour, for her English father had emigrated to Australia, married a Tasmanian, and made a fortune as a shipping merchant. But the whole family — father, mother and six children — returned to London in 1870; she was educated by a governess, in London and Lausanne, then at Queen's College, Acton, and finally at the Royal College of Music, where she studied piano and organ. Her legs were so short that she had a strenuous time reaching the pedals.

She was barely five feet tall, slim, blue-eyed, square-jawed, with a little wrinkle on her nose when she smiled. Her voice was high and soft, a sort of coo; E. M. Forster described it as a "society drawl". She had a very pretty elder sister under whose shadow her own prettiness seemed questionable. But she was stylish (her cousin Katherine Mansfield was to write, in 1921: "I have gathered Elizabeth's frocks to my bosom as if they were part of her flowers"). By that time everyone had adopted her alias and was calling her "Elizabeth". In her youth, and to her family, she was simply "May".

Her first husband, Henning von Arnim, called her "Dolly".

He met her in Italy in 1889. She was twenty-three and on an extended tour with her father; he was thirty-eight, travelling alone, seeking to recover from the deaths of his first wife and infant child. He heard the young English woman playing Bach fugues in the American church in Rome and quickly decided that she should be his second wife. He was himself a brilliant pianist — a pupil of Liszt. He was also a highly intelligent man, terse and authoritarian, the product of a paternalistic, *hoch geboren* society. He proposed to her several times, ignoring her refusals; finally Elizabeth gave way. She learnt German, they were married and a few years later he became the model for her comic creation: "The Man of Wrath".

He wanted an heir. For the first three successive years of their marriage, living in Berlin, she bore him daughters. Characteristically disregarding the true months of their births, she called them the April, May and June babies. But she was full of resentment at the enforced childbearing, while he was relentless in his continuing demands for a son. After prolonged hostility between them, Elizabeth produced a fourth daughter in 1899: she became pregnant while she was still writing *The Solitary Summer*.

But by then her life had changed for the better. They had moved to Nassenheide, one of the von Arnim family estates: a huge sixteenth-century house set in an immense, flat landscape of forests and water and fields of waving rye and sandy black roads, where the cranes flew crying through the sky in winter and butterflies danced over the fields in summer, and her love affair with a place and a garden began.

Like many love affairs, it involved a conflict. She wanted to be by herself there, she wanted to shed her clamouring domestic responsibilities and wander off with a book, to lie down on the mown grass beneath the bird-cherry trees. She wanted to get into the open basketwork carriage with scarlet wheels, her Great Dane, Ingraban, beside her, and be whirled through the woods by the faithful old coachman, sometimes even as far as the Baltic Sea. She did not want to spend her time distributing sausages and entertaining a stream of visitors.

Elizabeth was a prodigious reader. Temperamentally, she identified with the Romantic poets, particularly Wordsworth and Keats; but she knew her Spenser and Milton, her Goethe and Schiller. She read Thoreau and regarded him as a close but solemn friend whom she could tease. She also read Crabbe, Pater, Stevenson, Pepys, Boswell, Carlisle; the May 15th entry on her reading in *The Solitary Summer* is an elegant *tour de force*.

If you had encountered her in the garden when she hoped to be alone, she might have been icy. In *Elizabeth and Her German Garden* she had written witheringly of the unwanted persons who interrupted her private moments:

> I have been much afflicted again lately by visitors — not stray callers to be got rid of after due administration of tea and things you are sorry afterwards that you said, but people staying in the house and not to be got rid of at all . . . a garden where you meet the people you saw at breakfast, and will see again at lunch and dinner, is not a place to be happy in.

She was clever and an incorrigible tease. If she thought you stupid, or hidebound, she would make you shrivel under her contempt and impatience. But if you amused her she would be, in return, like a glass of champagne: sparkling, dry, lifting the present moment until it blotted out all humdrum anxieties and fears for the past and future, and leaving a sense of flatness behind her when she went away. Her father found in his "darling May", "a rare and fascinating combination of dove and serpent". E. M. Forster, who was English tutor to her children in 1904, rapidly decided that she was "most pleasant and amusing and I think I shall like her very much. She is, as I rather expected, nicer than her books, and I don't feel in awe of her." In the evenings at Nassenheide he found himself reading Jane Austen aloud to her.

One of his successors as English tutor to her children, Hugh Walpole, though terrified of her at first, became in later years her devoted fan: "I really like her better than any other woman alive," he wrote in 1919. "She has everything — brain, heart, humour, pluck." Two years later Katherine Mansfield wrote, in a letter to the painter, Brett: "the point about her is that one loves her and is proud of her."

Elizabeth did not love herself, and had a sharp line in self-ridicule. She presented herself as an ignorant and over-optimistic gardener, surrounded by mistakes and weeds. She was dismissive about her own writing and embarrassed if high claims were made for it. When she finished *The Solitary Summer* she recorded in her diary: "Read it through — mixed feelings — chiefly disgust. Futility that cannot be uttered." She told John Middleton Murry, after Katherine Mansfield's death — "I so longed for her not to mind me too much, not to find me out too completely." She wore a defensive armour against adverse criticism. She allows one of her early heroines, Fraülein Schmidt, to confess:

"I adore being praised. Dreadfully vain down in my heart, I go about pretending a fine aloofness from such weakness, so that when nobody sees anything in me — and nobody ever does — I may at least make a show of not having expected them to . . ."

Her pride, her scorn of self-pity, was part of the front which so intimidated the young Hugh Walpole in 1907 when he sat down at the Nassenheide luncheon table along with the German tutor, the German governess, the French governess, the four little girls, the little boy (for she had at last had a son), and the Count and Countess themselves. He distinguished three different modes in her behaviour:

(1) Charming, like her books only more so (this does not appear often).

(2) Ragging. Now she is unmerciful — attacks you on every side, goes at you until you are reduced to idiocy, and then drops you limp.

(3) Silence. This is the most terrible of all. She sits absolutely mute and if one tries to speak one gets snubbed.

The silent Elizabeth was, of course, the writer. She had come in from her *Treibhaus* — the high greenhouse where, behind long windows, she took to writing in the years after she scribbled *The Solitary Summer* in an upstairs room. Her mind was still full of her "stories", as she called them, when she came indoors; she could not handle lunchtime chat. She was a compulsive writer. As soon as she finished one book she embarked upon another. She turned her life into fiction as she went along, both simplifying and exaggerating the things that happened to her. Wherever she lived (and she was to live in many different houses and several different countries) there was always a little garden house where she worked, usually with a forbidding inscription over the door. Her children longed for her company but accepted her withdrawal from them; it had always been so. As one story succeeded another, she took to keeping regular, professional writing hours — hours which allowed her to emerge positively relaxed at lunchtime and able to join in her guests' conversation before disappearing again in the afternoons.

But in 1898, when Elizabeth was writing *The Solitary Summer*, there was no such luxury. The book was written patchily, and against the odds. The beautiful promise of summer weather in May that year was followed by ruinous screaming gales. She did not start writing until July, and in August she took the children away for a seaside holiday. In September her relations with her husband became so full of "wrath" that she took herself, alone, to England. When she returned to Nassenheide, she brought her sister and niece with her; she did not begin to write again until cold November; by December, she discovered her pregnancy with a heavy heart. But she finished the book in January, corrected the proofs in February, and

The Solitary Summer, light hearted and ebullient, was in the bookshops by the following May.

It is a series of essays — fluent and discursive, two for each month between May and October. So immediate is the sense of the present moment and of a speaking voice that it is hard to believe that these are not really entries from a journal. She moves into the present tense, a day is described; she walks through a ryefield with Thoreau under her arm, swishing a bunch of grass to and fro across her face to keep the flies away; she sits on the veranda, while the shadows of leaves dapple her page. The garden is never static, for the weather, the light, are always playing on it and she is moving through it. Most entries have the garden as their starting point — then evolve, seamlessly, into ironic discussion of human weaknesses, of unwanted social encounters, of sleep, or the weather, with satiric exchanges between herself and the 'Man of Wrath', and deadpan conversations about God, Heaven and Hell in which the April, May and June babies speak in baby broken English.

Her wide reading in English literature shows in her style, and her mastery of the loose, associative essay form reflects her admiration of Charles Lamb. She floats an idea: she would rather be a goose-girl than a countess. She praises geese — "delightfully plump, placid . . . their very waddle in its lazy deliberation soothing and salutary to a fretted spirit that has been too long on the stretch". But she passes easily on to a consideration of roast goose, stuffed with apple, and suddenly her attention is fixed on the little white hands and glittering rings of a noblewoman eating more than her share of crackling. This leads easily to a mockery of the German interest in food, *das Essen*, which carries her to the end of the chapter.

The finest passage in the book, however, is not discursive, but concentrated and intense. It describes the experience of walking alone through a dewy garden before dawn, and it is written in rhythmic prose that momentarily echoes the repetitive cadences of the seventeenth century. Very early one morning, between three o'clock and four, she unbolts the front door and drifts out in her dressing gown and slippers through "the greys and blues and faint pearly-whites" of the garden. The drawn blinds and closed shutters of the house are behind her:

> Here was the world wide-awake and yet only for me, all the fresh pure air only for me, all the fragrance breathed only by me, not a living soul hearing the nightingale but me, the sun in a few moments coming up to warm only me.

It is a celebration of solitude in a garden that alone justifies the title of the book. Elizabeth recreates a Wordsworthian sense of rapturous awe but, like Wordsworth, faithfully records the fact that she cannot hold onto it; unhappy thoughts assail her at the very moment when she had most expected ecstasy. She finds herself thinking instead of the awful isolation of each human soul: her longing for solitude metamorphosed into fear of black loneliness — a dichotomy that gave tension to the rest of Elizabeth's life.

The book is not really about solitude at all, but about the desire for solitude in someone who finds herself surrounded by people. There are servants demanding instructions, "the babies" with their cardboard boxes of snails, the army descending in force and requiring billets, and — always present in the background — the farm labourers, the poor. The whole entry for July 15th is devoted to the poor, and to Elizabeth's vain efforts at educative philanthropy; it sits oddly amongst the flippant charms of the rest of the book, but was written in response to reviews of *Elizabeth and Her German Garden* which complained of the author's selfishness. She was vulnerable to accusations like these. In the month of August she reports the fault-finding of a sanctimonious missionary, who chides her for being too happy:

> He pointed out that sorrow and sickness were sure to come — that all around me lay misery, sin, and suffering, and that every person not absolutely blinded by selfishness must be aware of it.

She was well aware of it. And sorrows did come to her in full measure as her life progressed: a miserable second marriage, the grievous deaths of a daughter, a brother. But she remained a steadfast hedonist, firmly suppressing sorrows. "Who wants to write, or think, of ancient griefs?" she asks in her comic autobiography, *All the Dogs of my Life*. Her journals and letters repeatedly record moments of happiness, usually associated with sunny days. "I'm so glad I didn't die on the various occasions I have earnestly wished I might," she wrote to her friend, Maud Ritchie, in 1921, "for if I had I would have missed a lot of lovely weather." In her last years she wrote to her beloved daughter Liebet (the May baby): "What I really am by nature is an escapist."

It was true. And all the heroines of her novels are escapists too. They escape from richness into the simple life, or from conventional home life into foreign travel; they escape from houses into caravans. Above all they escape, or need to escape, from husbands. Elizabeth saw marriage as a tyranny, husbands as tyrants, women as overdue for liberation.

In her first two books, the escape is simply into a garden set in a wide landscape. And it was her capacity to present her joy in the place that made the books bestsellers. Her readers were escaping, with her, into happiness.

Deborah Kellaway, London, 1992

May

MAY

May 2nd.—Last night after dinner, when we were in the garden, I said, "I want to be alone for a whole summer, and get to the very dregs of life. I want to be as idle as I can, so that my soul may have time to grow. Nobody shall be invited to stay with me, and if any one calls they will be told that I am out, or away, or sick. I shall spend the months in the garden, and on the plain, and in the forests. I shall watch the things that happen in my garden, and see where I have made mistakes. On wet days I will go into the thickest parts of the forests, where the pine needles are everlastingly dry, and when the sun shines I'll lie on the heath and see how the broom flares against the clouds. I shall be perpetually happy, because there will be no one to worry me. Out there on the plain there is silence, and where there is silence I have discovered there is peace."

"Mind you do not get your feet damp," said the Man of Wrath, removing his cigar.

It was the evening of May Day, and the spring had taken hold of me body and soul. The sky was full of stars, and the garden of scents, and the borders of wallflowers and sweet, sly pansies. All day there had been a breeze, and all day slow masses of white clouds had been sailing across the blue. Now it was so still, so motionless, so breathless, that it seemed as though a quiet hand had been laid on the garden, soothing and hushing it into silence.

The Man of Wrath sat at the foot of the verandah steps in that placid after-dinner mood which suffers fools, if not gladly, at least indulgently, and I stood in front of him, leaning against the sun-dial.

"Shall you take a book with you?" he asked.

"Yes, I shall," I replied, slightly nettled by his tone. "I am quite ready to admit that though the fields and flowers are always ready to teach, I am not always in the mood to learn, and sometimes my eyes are incapable of seeing things that at other times are quite plain."

" And then you read ? "

" And then I read. Well, dear Sage, what of that ? "

But he smoked in silence, and seemed suddenly absorbed by the stars.

"See," he said, after a pause, during which I stood looking at him and wishing he would use longer sentences, and he looked at the sky and did not think about me at all, " see how bright the stars are to-night. Almost as though it might freeze."

" It isn't going to freeze, and I won't look at anything until you have told me what you think of my idea. Wouldn't a whole lovely summer, quite alone, be delightful? Wouldn't it be perfect to get up every morning for weeks and feel that you belong to yourself and to nobody else ? " And I went over to him and put a hand on each shoulder and gave him a little shake, for he persisted in gazing at the stars just as though I had not been there. " Please, Man of Wrath, say something long for once," I entreated ; " you haven't said a good long sentence for a week."

He slowly brought his gaze from the stars down to me and smiled. Then he drew me on to his knee.

"Don't get affectionate," I urged ; "it is words, not deeds, that I want. But I'll stay here if you'll talk."

"Well then, I will talk. What am I to say ? You know you do as you please, and I never interfere with you. If you do not want to have any one here this summer you will not have any one, but you will find it a very long summer."

"No, I won't."

"And if you lie on the heath all day, people will think you are mad."

"What do I care what people think ?"

"No, that is true. But you will catch cold, and your little nose will swell."

"Let it swell."

"And when it is hot you will be sunburnt and your skin spoilt."

"I don't mind my skin."

"And you will be dull."

"Dull ?"

It often amuses me to reflect how very little the Man of Wrath really knows me. Here we have been three years buried in the country, and I as happy as a bird the whole time. I say as a bird, because other people have used the simile to describe absolute cheerfulness, although I do not believe birds are any happier than any one else, and they quarrel disgracefully. I have been as happy then, we will say, as the best of birds, and have had seasons of solitude at intervals before now during which dull is the last word to describe my state of mind. Everybody, it is true, would not like it, and I had some visitors here a fortnight ago who left after staying about a week and clearly not enjoying themselves. They found it dull, I know, but that of course was their own fault ; how can you make a person happy against his will ? You can knock a great deal into him in the way of learning and what the schools call extras, but if you try for ever you will not knock any happiness into a being who has not got it in him to be happy. The only result probably would be that you knock your own out of yourself. Obviously happiness must come from within, and not from without ; and judging from my past experience and my present sensations, I should say that I have a store just now within me more than sufficient to fill five quiet months.

"I wonder," I remarked after a pause, during which I began to suspect that I too must belong to the serried ranks of the *femmes incomprises*, "why you think I shall be dull. The garden is always beautiful, and I am nearly always in the mood to enjoy it. Not quite always, I must confess, for when those Schmidts were here" (their name was not Schmidt, but what does that matter?) "I grew almost to hate it. Whenever I went into it there they were, dragging themselves about with faces full of indignant resignation. Do you suppose they saw one of those blue hepaticas overflowing the shrubberies? And when I drove with them into the woods, where the fairies were so busy just then hanging the branches with little green jewels, they talked about Berlin the whole time, and the good savouries their new *chef* makes."

"Well, my dear, no doubt they missed their savouries. Your garden, I acknowledge, is growing very pretty, but your cook is bad. Poor Schmidt sometimes looked quite ill at dinner, and the beauty of your floral arrangements in no way made up for the inferior quality of the food. Send her away."

"Send her away? Be thankful you have her. A bad cook is more effectual a great deal than Kissingen and Carlsbad and Homburg rolled into one, and very much cheaper. As long as I have her, my dear man, you will be comparatively thin and amiable. Poor Schmidt, as you call him, eats too much of those delectable savouries, and then looks at his wife and wonders why he married her. Don't let me catch you doing that."

" I do not think it is very likely," said the Man of Wrath ; but whether he meant it prettily, or whether he was merely thinking of the improbability of his ever eating too much of the local savouries, I cannot tell. I object, however, to discussing cooks in the garden on a starlight night, so I got off his knee and proposed that we should stroll round a little.

It was such a sweet evening, such a fitting close to a beautiful May Day, and the flowers shone in the twilight like pale stars, and the air was full of fragrance, and I envied the bats fluttering through such a bath of scent, with the real stars above and the pansy stars beneath, and themselves so fashioned that even if they wanted to they could not make a noise and disturb the prevailing peace. A great deal that is poetical has been written by English people about May Day, and the impression left on the foreign mind is an impression of posies, and garlands, and village greens, and youths and maidens much be-ribboned, and lambs, and general friskiness. I was in England once on a May Day, and we sat over the fire shivering and listening blankly to the north-east wind tearing down the

street and the rattling of the hail against the
windows, and the friends with whom I was staying said it was very often so, and that they had
never seen any lambs and ribbons. We Germans
attach no poetical significance to it at all, and yet
we well might, for it is almost invariably beautiful ;
and as for garlands, I wonder how many villages
full of young people could have been provided
with them out of my garden, and nothing be
missed? It is to-day a garden of wallflowers, and
I think I have every colour and sort in cultivation.
The borders under the south windows of the house,
so empty and melancholy this time last year, are
crammed with them, and are finished off in front
by a broad strip from end to end of yellow and
white pansies. The tea rose beds round the sun-
dial facing these borders are sheets of white, and
golden, and purple, and wine-red pansies, with the
dainty red shoots of the tea roses presiding delicately in their midst. The verandah steps leading
down into this pansy paradise have boxes of white,
and pink, and yellow tulips all the way up on each
side, and on the lawn, behind the roses, are two
big beds of every coloured tulip rising above a
carpet of forget-me-nots. How very much more
charming different-coloured tulips are together

than tulips in one colour by itself! Last year, on the recommendation of sundry writers about gardens, I tried beds of scarlet tulips and forget-me-nots. They were pretty enough ; but I wish those writers could see my beds of mixed tulips. I never saw anything so sweetly, delicately gay The only ones I exclude are the rose-coloured ones ; but scarlet, gold, delicate pink, and white are all there, and the effect is infinitely enchanting. The forget-me-nots grow taller as the tulips go off, and will presently tenderly engulf them altogether, and so hide the shame of their decay in their kindly little arms. They will be left there, clouds of gentle blue, until the tulips are well withered, and then they will be taken away to make room for the scarlet geraniums that are to occupy these two beds in the summer and flare in the sun as much as they like. I love an occasional mass of fiery colour, and these two will make the lilies look even whiter and more breathless that are to stand sentinel round the semicircle containing the precious tea roses.

The first two years I had this garden I was determined to do exactly as I chose in it, and to have no arrangements of plants that I had not planned, and no plants but those I knew and loved ;

so, fearing that an experienced gardener would profit by my ignorance, then about as absolute as it could be, and thrust all his bedding nightmares upon me, and fill the place with those dreadful salad arrangements so often seen in the gardens of the indifferent rich, I would only have a meek man of small pretensions, who would be easily persuaded that I knew as much as, or more than, he did himself. I had three of these meek men one after the other, and learned what I might long ago have discovered, that the less a person knows, the more certain he is that he is right, and that no weapons yet invented are of any use in a struggle with stupidity. The first of these three went melancholy mad at the end of a year; the second was love-sick, and threw down his tools and gave up his situation to wander after the departed siren who had turned his head; the third, when I inquired how it was that the things he had sown never by any chance came up, scratched his head, and as this is a sure sign of ineptitude I sent him away.

Then I sat down and thought. I had been here two years and worked hard, through these men, at the garden; I had done my best to learn all I could and make it beautiful; I had refused to have more than an inferior gardener

because of his supposed more perfect obedience,
and one assistant, because of my desire to enjoy
the garden undisturbed ; I had studied diligently
all the gardening books I could lay hands on ; I
was under the impression that I am an ordinarily
intelligent person, and that if an ordinarily
intelligent person devotes his whole time to
studying a subject he loves, success is very
probable ; and yet at the end of two years what
was my garden like ? The failures of the first
two summers had been regarded with philosophy ;
but that third summer I used to go into it sometimes and cry.

As far as I was concerned I had really learned
a little, and knew what to buy, and had fairly
correct notions as to when and in what soil to
sow and plant what I had bought ; but of
what use is it to buy good seeds and plants and
bulbs if you are forced to hand them over to a
gardener who listens with ill-concealed impatience
to the careful directions you give him, says
Jawohl a great many times, and then goes off
and puts them in in the way he has always done,
which is invariably the wrong way ? My hands
were tied because of the unfortunate circumstance
of sex, or I would gladly have changed places

with him and requested him to do the talking while I did the planting, and as he probably would not have talked much there would have been a distinct gain in the peace of the world, which would surely be very materially increased if women's tongues were tied instead of their hands, and those that want to could work with them without collecting a crowd. And is it not certain that the more one's body works the fainter grow the waggings of one's tongue? I sometimes literally ache with envy as I watch the men going about their pleasant work in the sunshine, turning up the luscious damp earth, raking, weeding, watering, planting, cutting the grass, pruning the trees—not a thing that they do from the first uncovering of the roses in the spring to the November bonfires but fills my soul with longing to be up and doing it too. A great many things will have to happen, however, before such a state of popular large-mindedness as will allow of my digging without creating a sensation is reached, so I have plenty of time for further grumblings; only I do very much wish that the tongues inhabiting this apparently lonely and deserted countryside would restrict their comments to the sins, if any, committed by the indigenous

females (since sins are fair game for comment)
and leave their harmless eccentricities alone.
After having driven through vast tracts of forest
and heath for hours, and never meeting a soul
or seeing a house, it is surprising to be told that
on such a day you took such a drive and were at
such a spot; yet this has happened to me more
than once. And if even this is watched and
noted, with what lightning rapidity would the
news spread that I had been seen stalking down
the garden path with a hoe over my shoulder
and a basket in my hand, and weeding written
large on every feature! Yet I should love to
weed.

I think it was the way the weeds flourished
that put an end at last to my hesitations about
taking an experienced gardener and giving him a
reasonable number of helpers, for I found that
much as I enjoyed privacy, I yet detested nettles
more, and the nettles appeared really to pick out
those places to grow in where my sweetest things
were planted, and utterly defied the three meek
men when they made periodical and feeble efforts
to get rid of them. I have a large heart in regard
to things that grow, and many a weed that would
not be tolerated anywhere else is allowed to live

and multiply undisturbed in my garden. They are such pretty things, some of them, such charmingly audacious things, and it is so particularly nice of them to do all their growing, and flowering, and seed-bearing without any help or any encouragement. I admit I feel vexed if they are so officious as to push up among my tea roses and pansies, and I also prefer my paths without them; but on the grass, for instance, why not let the poor little creatures enjoy themselves quietly, instead of going out with a dreadful instrument and viciously digging them up one by one? Once I went into the garden just as the last of the three inept ones had taken up his stand, armed with this implement, in the middle of the sheet of gold and silver that is known for convenience' sake as the lawn, and was scratching his head, as he looked round, in a futile effort to decide where he should begin. I saved the dandelions and daisies on that occasion, and I like to believe they know it. They certainly look very jolly when I come out, and I rather fancy the dandelions dig each other in their little ribs when they see me, and whisper, "Here comes Elizabeth; she's a good sort, ain't she?"—for of course dandelions do not express themselves very elegantly.

But nettles are not to be tolerated. They settled the question on which I had been turning my back for so long, and one fine August morning, when there seemed to be nothing in the garden but nettles, and it was hard to believe that we had ever been doing anything but carefully cultivating them in all their varieties, I walked into the Man of Wrath's den.

"My dear man," I began, in the small caressing voice of one who has long been obstinate and is in the act of giving in, "will you kindly advertise for a head gardener and a proper number of assistants? Nearly all the bulbs and seeds and plants I have squandered my money and my hopes on have turned out to be nettles, and I don't like them. I have had a wretched summer, and never want to see a meek gardener again."

"My dear Elizabeth," he replied, "I regret that you did not take my advice sooner. How often have I pointed out the folly of engaging one incapable person after the other? The vegetables, when we get any, are uneatable, and there is never any fruit. I do not in the least doubt your good intentions, but you are wanting in judgment. When will you learn to rely on my experience?"

I hung my head; for was he not in the

pleasant position of being able to say, "I told you so?"—which indeed he has been saying for the last two years. "I don't like relying," I murmured, "and have rather a prejudice against somebody else's experience. Please will you send the advertisement to-day?"

They came in such shoals that half the population must have been head gardeners out of situations. I took all the likely ones round the garden, and I do not think I ever spent a more chastening week than that week of selection. Their remarks were, naturally, of the frankest nature, as I had told them I had had practically only gardeners' assistants since I lived here, and they had no idea, when they were politely scoffing at some arrangement, that it happened to be one of my own. The hot-beds in the kitchen garden with which I had taken such pains were objects of special derision. It appeared that they were all wrong—measurements, preparation, soil, manure, everything that could be wrong, was. Certainly the only crop we had from them was weeds. But I began about half way through the week to grow sceptical, because on comparing their criticisms I found they seldom agreed, and so took courage again. Finally I chose a nice, trim young man, with

strikingly intelligent eyes and quick movements,
who had shown himself less concerned with the
state of chaos existing than with considerations of
what might eventually be made of the place. He
is very deaf, so he wastes no time in words, and is
exceedingly keen on gardening, and knows, as I
very soon discovered, a vast amount more than I
do, in spite of my three years' application. More-
over, he is filled with that humility and eagerness
to learn which is only found in those who have
already learned more than their neighbours. He
enters into my plans with enthusiasm, and makes
suggestions of his own, which, if not always quite
in accordance with what are perhaps my peculiar
tastes, at least plainly show that he understands
his business. We had a very busy winter together
altering all the beds, for they none of them had
been given a soil in which plants could grow, and
next autumn I intend to have all the so-called
lawns dug up and levelled, and shall see whether
I cannot have decent turf here. I told him he
must save the daisy and dandelion roots, and he
looked rather crestfallen at that, but he is young,
and can learn to like what I like, and get rid of
his only fault, a nursery-gardener attitude towards
all flowers that are not the fashion. " I shall want

a great many daffodils next spring," I shouted **one** day at the beginning of our acquaintance.

His eyes gleamed. "Ah yes," he said with immediate approval, "they are *sehr modern*."

I was divided between amusement at the notion of Spenser's daffadowndillies being *modern*, and indignation at hearing exactly the same adjective applied to them that the woman who sells me my hats bestows on the most appalling examples of her stock.

"They are to be in troops on the grass," I said ; whereupon his face grew doubtful. "That is indeed *sehr modern*," I shouted. But he had grown suddenly deafer — a phenomenon I have observed to occur every time my orders are such as he has never been given before. After a time he will, I think, become imbued with my unorthodoxy in these matters ; and meanwhile he has the true gardening spirit and loves his work, and love, after all, is the chief thing. I know of no compost so good. In the poorest soil, love alone, by itself, will work wonders.

Down the garden path, past the copse of lilacs with their swelling dark buds, and the great three-cornered bed of tea roses and pansies in front of it, between the rows of china roses and past the lily and foxglove groups, we came last night to the spring garden in the open glade round the old oak ; and there, the first to flower of the flowering trees, and standing out like a lovely white naked thing against the dusk of the evening, was a double cherry in full bloom, while close beside it, but not so visible so late, with all their graceful growth outlined by rosy buds, were two Japanese crab apples. The grass just there is filled with narcissus, and at the foot of the oak a colony of tulips consoles me for the loss of the purple crocus patches, so lovely a little while since.

"I must be by myself for once a whole summer through," I repeated, looking round at these things with a feeling of hardly being able to bear their beauty, and the beauty of the starry sky, and the beauty of the silence and the scent—"I must be alone, so that I shall not miss one of these wonders, and have leisure really to *live*."

"Very well, my dear," replied the Man of Wrath, "only do not grumble afterwards when you find it dull. You shall be solitary if you choose, and, as far as I am concerned, I will invite no one. It is always best to allow a woman to do as she likes if you can, and it saves a good deal of bother. To have what she desired is generally an effective punishment."

"Dear Sage," I cried, slipping my hand through his arm, "don't be so wise! I promise you that I won't be dull, and I won't be punished, and I will be happy."

And we sauntered slowly back to the house in great contentment, discussing the firmament and such high things, as though we knew all about them.

May 15th. — There is a dip in the rye-fields about half a mile from my garden gate, a little round hollow like a dimple, with water and reeds at the bottom, and a few water-loving trees and bushes on the shelving ground around. Here I have been nearly every morning lately, for it suits the mood I am in, and I like the narrow footpath to it through the rye, and I like its solitary dampness in a place where everything is parched, and when I am lying on the grass and look down I can see the reeds glistening greenly in the water, and when I look up I can see the rye-fringe brushing the sky. All sorts of beasts come and stare at me, and larks sing above me, and creeping things crawl over me, and stir in the long grass beside me ; and here I bring my book, and read and dream away the profitable morning hours, to the accompaniment of the amorous croakings of innumerable frogs.

Thoreau has been my companion for some days past, it having struck me as more appropriate to bring him out to a pond than to read him, as was hitherto my habit, on Sunday mornings in the garden. He is a person who loves the open air, and will refuse to give you much pleasure if you try to read him amid the pomp and circumstance of upholstery; but out in the sun, and especially by this pond, he is delightful, and we spend the happiest hours together, he making statements, and I either agreeing heartily, or just laughing and reserving my opinion till I shall have more ripely considered the thing. He, of course, does not like me as much as I like him, because I live in a cloud of dust and germs produced by wilful superfluity of furniture, and have not the courage to get a match and set light to it; and every day he sees the door-mat on which I wipe my shoes on going into the house, in defiance of his having told me that he had once refused the offer of one on the ground that it is best to avoid even the beginnings of evil. But my philosophy has not yet reached the acute stage that will enable me to see a door-mat in its true character as a hinderer of the development of souls, and I like to wipe my shoes. Perhaps if I had to live with few servants, or if it were possible, short of existence in a cave, to do without them altogether, I should also do without door-mats, and probably in summer without shoes too, and wipe my feet on the grass nature no doubt provides for this purpose; and meanwhile we know that though he went to the woods, Thoreau came back again, and lived for the rest of his days like other people. During his life, I imagine he would have refused to notice anything so fatiguing as an ordinary German woman, and never would have deigned discourse to me on the themes he loved best; but now his spirit belongs to me, and all he thought, and believed, and felt, and he talks as much and as intimately to me here in my solitude as ever he did to his dearest friends years ago in Concord. In the garden he was a pleasant companion, but in the lonely dimple he is fascinating, and the morning hours hurry past at a quite surprising rate when he is with me, and it grieves me to be obliged to interrupt him in the middle of some quaint sentence or beautiful thought just because the sun is touching a certain

bush down by the water's edge, which is a sign
that it is lunch-time and that I must be off.
Back we go together through the rye, he carefully
tucked under one arm, while with the other I
brandish a bunch of grass to keep off the flies that
appear directly we emerge into the sunshine.
"Oh, my dear Thoreau," I murmur sometimes,
overcome by the fierce heat of the little path
at noonday and the persistence of the flies, "did
you have flies at Walden to exasperate you?
And what became of your philosophy then?"
But he never notices my plaints, and I know that
inside his covers he is discoursing away like anything on the folly of allowing oneself to be over-
whelmed in that terrible rapid and whirlpool
called a dinner, which is situated in the meridian
shallows, and of the necessity, if one would keep
happy, of sailing by it looking another way,
tied to the mast like Ulysses. But he gets grimly
carried back for all that, and is taken into the
house and put on his shelf and left there, because
I still happen to have a body attached to my
spirit, which, if not fed at the ordinary time,
becomes a nuisance. Yet he is right; luncheon
is a snare of the tempter, and I would perhaps try
to sail by it like Ulysses if I had a biscuit in my

pocket to comfort me, but there are the babies to
be fed, and the Man of Wrath, and how can a
respectable wife and mother sail past any meridian
shallows in which those dearest to her have stuck?
So I stand by them, and am punished every day
by that two-o'clock-in-the-afternoon feeling to
which I so much object, and yet cannot avoid.
It is mortifying, after the sunshiny morning
hours at my pond, when I feel as though I were
almost a poet, and very nearly a philosopher, and
wholly a joyous animal in an ecstasy of love with
life, to come back and live through those dreary
luncheon-ridden hours, when the soul is crushed
out of sight and sense by cutlets and asparagus
and revengeful sweet things. My morning friend
turns his back on me when I re-enter the library;
nor do I ever touch him in the afternoon. Books
have their idiosyncrasies as well as people, and
will not show me their full beauties unless the
place and time in which they are read suits them.
If, for instance, I cannot read Thoreau in a
drawing-room, how much less would I ever dream
of reading Boswell in the grass by a pond!
Imagine carrying him off in company with his
great friend to a lonely dell in a rye-field, and
expecting them to be entertaining. " Nay, my dear

lady," the great man would say in mighty tones of rebuke, " this will never do. Lie in a rye-field? What folly is that? And who would converse in a damp hollow that can help it?" So I read and laugh over my Boswell in the library when the lamps are lit, buried in cushions and surrounded by every sign of civilisation, with the drawn curtains shutting out the garden and the country solitude so much disliked by both sage and disciple. Indeed, it is Bozzy who asserts that in the country the only things that make one happy are meals. "I was happy," he says, when stranded at a place called Corrichatachin in the Island of Skye, and unable to get out of it because of the rain, " I was happy when tea came. Such I take it is the state of those who live in the country. Meals are wished for from the cravings of vacuity of mind, as well as from the desire of eating." And such is the perverseness of human nature that Boswell's wisdom delights me even more than Johnson's, though I love them both very heartily.

In the afternoon I potter in the garden with Goethe. He did not, I am sure, care much really about flowers and gardens, yet he said many lovely things about them that remain in one's memory

just as persistently as though they had been
inspired expressions of actual feelings ; and the
intellect must indeed have been gigantic that could
so beautifully pretend.   Ordinary blunderers have
to feel a vast amount before they can painfully
stammer out a sentence that will describe it ; and
when they have got it out, how it seems to have
just missed the core of the sensation that gave it
birth, and what a poor, weak child it is of what
was perhaps a mighty feeling! I read Goethe
on a special seat, never departed from when he
accompanies me, a seat on the south side of an
ice-house, and thus sheltered from the north winds
sometimes prevalent in May, and shaded by the
low-hanging branches of a great beech-tree from
more than flickering sunshine.   Through these
branches I can see a group of giant poppies just
coming into flower, flaming out beyond the trees
on the grass, and farther down a huge silver
birch, its first spring green not yet deepened out
of delicacy, and looking almost golden backed by
a solemn cluster of firs.   Here I read Goethe—
everything I have of his, both what is well known
and what is not ; here I shed invariable tears over
Werther, however often I read it ; here I wade
through *Wilhelm Meister*, and sit in amazement

before the complications of the *Wahlverwand-schaften*; here I am plunged in wonder and wretchedness by *Faust*; and here I sometimes walk up and down in the shade and apostrophise the tall firs at the bottom of the glade in the opening soliloquy of *Iphigenia*. Every now and then I leave the book on the seat and go and have a refreshing potter among my flower beds, from which I return greatly benefited, and with a more just conception of what, in this world, is worth bothering about, and what is not.

In the evening, when everything is tired and quiet, I sit with Walt Whitman by the rose beds and listen to what that lonely and beautiful spirit has to tell me of night, sleep, death, and the stars. This dusky, silent hour is his; and this is the time when I can best hear the beatings of that most tender and generous heart. Such great love, such rapture of jubilant love for nature, and the good green grass, and trees, and clouds, and sunlight; such aching anguish of love for all that breathes and is sick and sorry; such passionate longing to help and mend and comfort that which never can be helped and mended and comforted; such eager looking to death, delicate death, as the one complete and final consolation—before this revelation

of yearning, universal pity, every-day selfishness
stands awe-struck and ashamed.

When I drive in the forests, Keats goes with
me ; and if I extend my drive to the Baltic shores,
and spend the afternoon on the moss beneath the
pines whose pink stems form the framework of the
sea, I take Spenser ; and presently the blue waves
are the ripples of the Idle Lake, and a tiny white
sail in the distance is Phaedria's shallow ship, bearing Cymochles swiftly away to her drowsy little nest
of delights.   How can I tell why Keats has never
been brought here, and why Spenser is brought
again and again ? Who shall follow the dark
intricacies of the elementary female mind?   It is
safer not to attempt to do so, but by simply cata-
loguing them collectively under the heading Instinct,
have done with them once and for all.

What a blessing it is to love books. Everybody must love something, and I know of no
objects of love that give such substantial and
unfailing returns as books and a garden.   And
how easy it would have been to come into the
world without this, and possessed instead of an
all - consuming passion, say, for hats, perpetually raging round my empty soul ! I feel I owe
my forefathers a debt of gratitude, for I suppose

the explanation is that they too did not care for
hats.   In the centre of my library there is a wooden
pillar propping up the ceiling, and preventing it,
so I am told, from tumbling about our ears ; and
round this pillar, from floor to ceiling, I have had
shelves fixed, and on these shelves are all the books
that I have read again and again, and hope to read
many times more—all the books, that is, that I
love quite the best.   In the bookcases round the
walls are many that I love, but here in the centre
of the room, and easiest to get at, are those I love
the *best*—the very elect among my favourites.
They change from time to time as I get older, and
with years some that are in the bookcases come
here, and some that are here go into the bookcases, and some again are removed altogether, and
are placed on certain shelves in the drawing-room
which are reserved for those that have been weighed
in the balance and found wanting, and from
whence they seldom, if ever, return.   Carlyle used
to be among the elect.   That was years ago, when
my hair was very long, and my skirts very short,
and I sat in the paternal groves with *Sartor
Resartus*, and felt full of wisdom and *Weltschmerz* ;
and even after I was married, when we lived in
town, and the noise of his thunderings was almost

drowned by the rattle of droschkies over the stones in the street below, he still shone forth a bright, particular star. Now, whether it is age creeping upon me, or whether it is that the country is very still and sound carries, or whether my ears have grown sensitive, I know not ; but the moment I open him there rushes out such a clatter of denunciation, and vehemence, and wrath, that I am completely deafened ; and as I easily get bewildered, and love peace, and my chief aim is to follow the apostle's advice and study to be quiet, he has been degraded from his high position round the pillar and has gone into retirement against the wall, where the accident of alphabet causes him to rest in the soothing society of one Carina, a harmless gentleman, whose book on the *Bagni di Lucca* is on his left, and a Frenchman of the name of Charlemagne, whose soporific comedy written at the beginning of the century and called *Le Testament de l'Oncle, ou Les Lunettes Cassées*, is next to him on his right. Two works of his still remain, however, among the elect, though differing in glory—his *Frederick the Great*, fascinating for obvious reasons to the patriotic German mind, and his *Life of Sterling*, a quiet book on the whole, a record of an uneventful life, in which the natural

positions of subject and biographer are reversed,
the man of genius writing the life of the unim-
portant friend, and the fact that the friend was
exceedingly lovable in no way lessening one's dis-
comfort in the face of such an anomaly. Carlyle
stands on an eminence altogether removed from
Sterling, who stands, indeed, on no eminence at
all, unless it be an eminence, that (happily) crowded
bit of ground, where the bright and courageous
and lovable stand together. We Germans have all
heard of Carlyle, and many of us have read him
with due amazement, our admiration often interrupted by groans at the difficulties his style places
in the candid foreigner's path ; but without Carlyle which of us would ever have heard of Sterling?
And even in this comparatively placid book
mines of the accustomed vehemence are sprung on
the shrinking reader. To the prosaic German,
nourished on a literature free from thunderings
and any marked acuteness of enthusiasm, Carlyle
is an altogether astonishing phenomenon.

And here I feel constrained to inquire sternly
who I am that I should talk in this unbecom-
ing manner of Carlyle? To which I reply that I
am only a humble German seeking after peace,
devoid of the least real desire to criticise anybody,

and merely anxious to get out of the way of
geniuses when they make too much noise. All I
want is to read quietly the books that I at present
prefer. Carlyle is shut up now and therefore
silent on his comfortable shelf ; yet who knows
but what in my old age, when I begin to feel really
young, I may not once again find comfort in him ?

What a medley of books there is round my
pillar ! Here is Jane Austen leaning against
Heine—what would she have said to that, I
wonder ?—with Miss Mitford and *Cranford* to
keep her in countenance on her other side. Here
is my Goethe, one of many editions I have of
him, the one that has made the acquaintance of
the ice-house and the poppies. Here are Ruskin,
Lubbock, White's *Selborne*, Izaak Walton, Drum-
mond, Herbert Spencer (only as much of him as
I hope I understand and am afraid I do not), Walter
Pater, Matthew Arnold, Thoreau, Lewis Carroll,
Oliver Wendell Holmes, Hawthorne, *Wuthering
Heights*, Lamb's *Essays*, Johnson's *Lives*, Marcus
Aurelius, Montaigne, Gibbon, the immortal Pepys,
the egregious Boswell, various American children's
books that I loved as a child and read and love
to this day ; various French children's books,
loved for the same reason ; whole rows of German

children's books, on which I was brought up, with their charming woodcuts of quaint little children in laced bodices, and good housemothers cutting bread and butter, and descriptions of the atmosphere of fearful innocence and pure religion and swift judgments and rewards in which they lived, and how the *Finger Gottes* was impressed on everything that happened to them ; all the poets ; most of the dramatists ; and, I verily believe, every gardening book and book about gardens that has been published of late years.

These gardening books are an unfailing delight, especially in winter, when to sit by my blazing peat fire with the snow driving past the windows and read the luscious descriptions of roses and all the other summer glories is one of my greatest pleasures. And then how well I get to know and love those gardens whose gradual development has been described by their owners, and how happily I wander in fancy down the paths of certain specially charming ones in Lancashire, Berkshire, Surrey, and Kent, and admire the beautiful arrangement of bed and border, and the charming bits in unexpected corners, and all the evidences of untiring love! Any book I see advertised that treats of gardens I immediately buy, and thus possess quite a collection of fascinating and instructive garden literature. A few are feeble, and get shunted off into the drawing-room; but the others stay with me winter and summer, and soon lose the gloss of their new coats, and put on the comfortable look of old friends in every-day clothes, under the frequent touch of affection. They are such special friends that I can hardly pass them without a nod and a smile at the well-known covers, each of which has some pleasant association of time and place to make it still more dear.

My spirit too has wandered in one or two French gardens, but has not yet heard of a German one loved beyond everything by its owner. It is, of course, possible that my countrymen do love them and keep quiet about them, but many things are possible that are not probable, and experience compels me to the opinion that this is one of them. We have the usual rich man who has fine gardens laid out regardless of expense, but those are not gardens in the sense I mean; and we have the poor man with his bit of ground, hardly ever treated otherwise than as a fowl-run or a place dedicated to potatoes; and as for the middle class, it is too busy hurrying through life

to have time or inclination to stop and plant a
rose.

How glad I am I need not hurry. What
a waste of life, just getting and spending. Sitting
by my pansy beds, with the slow clouds floating
leisurely past, and all the clear day before me, I
look on at the hot scramble for the pennies of
existence and am lost in wonder at the vulgarity
that pushes, and cringes, and tramples, untiring
and unabashed. And when you have got your
pennies, what then? They are only pennies, after
all—unpleasant, battered copper things, without
a gold piece among them, and never worth the
degradation of self, and the hatred of those below
you who have fewer, and the derision of those
above you who have more. And as I perceive I
am growing wise, and what is even worse, alle-
gorical, and as these are tendencies to be fought
against as long as possible, I'll go into the garden
and play with the babies, who at this moment are
sitting in a row on the buttercups, singing what
appear to be selections from popular airs.

June

JUNE

June 3rd.—The Man of Wrath, I observe, is laying traps for me and being deep. He has prophesied that I will find solitude intolerable, and he is naturally desirous that his prophecy should be fulfilled. He knows that continuous rain depresses me, and he is awaiting a spell of it to bring me to a confession that I was wrong after all, whereupon he will make that remark so precious to the married heart, " My dear, I told you so." He begins the day by tapping the barometer, looking at the sky, and shaking his head. If there are any clouds he remarks that they are coming up, and if there are none he says it is too fine to last. He has even gone the length once or twice of starting off to the farm on hot, sunny mornings in his mackintosh,

in order to impress on me beyond all doubt that
the weather is breaking up.   He studiously keeps
out of my way all day, so that I may have every
opportunity of being bored as quickly as possible,
and in the evenings he retires to his den directly
after dinner, muttering something about letters.
When he has finally disappeared, I go out to the
stars and laugh at his transparent wiles.

But how would it be if we did have a spell of
wet weather? I do not quite know.   As long as
it is fine, rainy days in the future do not seem so
very terrible, and one, or even two really wet
ones are quite enjoyable when they do come—
pleasant times that remind one of the snug winter
now so far off, times of reading, and writing, and
paying one's bills.   I never pay bills or write
letters on fine summer days.   Not for any one will
I forego all that such a day rightly spent out of
doors might give me ; so that a wet day at
intervals is almost as necessary for me as for my
garden.   But how would it be if there were many
wet days? I believe a week of steady drizzle in
summer is enough to make the stoutest heart
depressed.   It is to be borne in winter by the
simple expedient of turning your face to the fire ;
but when you have no fire, and very long days,

your cheerfulness slowly slips away, and the dreariness prevailing out of doors comes in and broods in the blank corners of your heart. I rather fancy, however, that it is a waste of energy to ponder over what I should do if we had a wet summer on such a radiant day as this. I prefer sitting here on the verandah and looking down through a frame of leaves at all the rosebuds June has put in the beds round the sun-dial, to ponder over nothing, and just be glad that I am alive. The verandah at two o'clock on a summer's afternoon is a place in which to be happy and not decide anything, as my friend Thoreau told me of some other tranquil spot this morning. The chairs are comfortable, there is a table to write on, and the shadows of young leaves flicker across the paper. On one side a Crimson Rambler is thrusting inquisitive shoots through the wooden bars, being able this year for the first time since it was planted to see what I am doing up here, and next to it a Jackmanni clematis clings with soft young fingers to anything it thinks likely to help it up to the goal of its ambition, the roof. I wonder which of the two will get there first. Down there in the rose beds, among the hundreds of buds there is only one full-blown rose as yet, a Marie van

Houtte, one of the loveliest of the tea roses, perfect
in shape and scent and colour, and in my garden
always the first rose to flower ; and the first flowers
it bears are the loveliest of its own lovely flowers,
as though it felt that the first of its children to see
the sky and the sun and the familiar garden after
the winter sleep ought to put on the very daintiest
clothes they can muster for such a festal occasion.

Through the open schoolroom windows I can
hear the two eldest babies at their lessons. The
village schoolmaster comes over every afternoon
and teaches them for two hours, so that we are
free from governesses in the house, and once those
two hours are over they are free for twenty-four
from anything in the shape of learning. The
schoolroom is next to the verandah, and as two
o'clock approaches their excitement becomes more
and more intense, and they flutter up and down
the steps, looking in their white dresses like angels
on a Jacob's ladder, or watch eagerly among the
bushes for a first glimpse of him, like miniature and
perfectly proper Isoldes. He is a kind giant
with that endless supply of patience so often
found in giants, especially when they happen to
be village schoolmasters, and judging from the
amount of laughter I hear, the babies seem to enjoy

their lessons in a way they never did before
Every day they prepare bouquets for him, and he
gets more of them than a *prima donna*, or at any
rate a more regular supply. The first day he
came I was afraid they would be very shy of such
a big strange man, and that he would extract
nothing from them but tears ; but the moment I
left them alone together and as I shut the door,
I heard them eagerly informing him, by way of
opening the friendship, that their heads were
washed every Saturday night, and that their hair-
ribbons did not match because there had not been
enough of the one sort to go round. I went away
hoping that they would not think it necessary to
tell him how often my head is washed, or any
other news of a personal nature about me ; but I
believe by this time that man knows everything
there is to know about the details of my morning
toilet, which is daily watched with the greatest
interest by the Three. I hope he will be more
successful than I was in teaching them Bible
stories. I never got farther than Noah, at which
stage their questions became so searching as to
completely confound me ; and as no one likes
being confounded, and it is especially regrettable
when a parent is placed in such a position, I

brought the course to an abrupt end by assuming
that owl-like air of wisdom peculiar to infallibility
in a corner, and telling them that they were too
young to understand these things for the present;
and they, having a touching faith in the truth of
every word I say, gave three contented little purrs
of assent, and proposed that we should play
instead at rolling down the grass bank under the
south windows—which I did not do, I am glad
to remember.

But the schoolmaster, after four weeks' teaching, has got them as far as Moses, and safely past
the Noah's ark on which I came to grief, and if
glibness is a sign of knowledge then they have
learned the story very thoroughly. Yesterday,
after he had gone, they emerged into the verandah
fresh from Moses and bursting with eagerness to
tell me all about it.

" Herr Schenk told us to-day about Moses,"
began the April baby, making a rush at me.

" Oh ? "

" Yes, and a *böser, böser König* who said
every boy must be deaded, and Moses was the
allerliebster."

" Talk English, my *dear* baby, and not such a
dreadful mixture," I besought.

"He wasn't a cat."

"A cat?"

"Yes, he wasn't a cat, that Moses—a boy was he."

"But of course he wasn't a cat," I said with some severity; "no one ever supposed he was."

"Yes, but mummy," she explained eagerly, with much appropriate hand-action, "the cook's Moses *is* a cat."

"Oh, I see. Well?"

"And he was put in a basket in the water, and that did swim. And then one time they comed, and she said——"

"Who came? And who said?"

"Why, the ladies; and the *Königstochter* said, ' *Ach hörmal, da schreit so etwas.* '"

"In German?"

"Yes, and then they went near, and one must take off her shoes and stockings and go in the water and fetch that tiny basket, and then they made it open, and that *Kind* did cry and cry and *strampel* so—" here both the babies gave such a vivid illustration of the *strampeln* that the verandah shook—"and see! it is a tiny baby. And they fetched somebody to give it to eat, and the *Königstochter* can keep that boy, and further it doesn't go."

"Do you love Moses, mummy?" asked the May baby, jumping into my lap, and taking my face in both her hands—one of the many pretty, caressing little ways of a very pretty, caressing little creature.

"Yes," I replied bravely, "I love him."

"Then I too!" they cried with simultaneous gladness, the seal having thus been affixed to the legitimacy of their regard for him. To be of such authority that your verdict on every subject under heaven is absolute and final is without doubt to be in a proud position, but, like all proud positions, it bristles with pitfalls and drawbacks to the weak-kneed ; and most of my conversations with the babies end in a sudden change of subject made necessary by the tendency of their remarks and the unanswerableness of their arguments.   Happily, yesterday the Moses talk was brought to an end by the April baby herself, who suddenly remembered that I had not yet seen and sympathised with her dearest possession, a Dutch doll called Mary Jane, since a lamentable accident had bereft it of both its legs ; and she had dived into the schoolroom and fished it out of the dark corner reserved for the mangled and thrust it in my face before I had well done musing on the nature and extent of my love for Moses—for I try to be conscientious—and bracing myself to meet the next question.

"See this poor Mary Jane," she said, her voice and hand quivering with tenderness as she lifted its petticoats to show me the full extent of the calamity, "see, mummy, no legs—only twowsers and nothing further."

I wish they would speak English a little better. The pains I take to correct them and weed out the German words that crop up in every sentence are really untiring, and the results discouraging. Indeed, as they get older the German asserts itself more and more, and is threatening to swallow up the little English they have left entirely. I talk English steadily with them, but everybody else, including a small French nurse lately imported, nothing but German. Somebody told me the thing to do was to let children pick up languages when they were babies, at which period they absorb them as easily as food and drink, and are quite unaware that they are learning anything at all; whereupon I immediately introduced this French girl into the family, forgetting how little

English they have absorbed, and the result has been that they pass their days delightfully in teaching her German. They were astonished at first on discovering that she could not understand a word they said, and soon set about altering such an uncomfortable state of things; and as they are three to one and very zealous, and she is a meek little person with a profile like a teapot with a twisted black handle of hair, their success was practically certain from the beginning, and she is getting on quite nicely with her German, and has at least already thoroughly learned all the mistakes. She wanders in the garden with a surprised look on her face as of one who is moving about in worlds not realised; and the three cling to her skirts and give her enthusiastic lessons all day long.

Poor Séraphine! What courage to weigh anchor at eighteen and go into a foreign country, to a place where you are among utter strangers, without a friend, unable to speak a word of the language, and not even sure before you start whether you will be given enough to eat. Either it is that saddest of courage forced on the timid by necessity, or, as Doctor Johnson would probably have said, it is stark insensibility; and I am afraid when I look at her I silently agree with the apostle

of common sense, and take it for granted that she
is incapable of deep feeling, for the altogether
inadequate reason that she has a certain resem-
blance to a teapot. Now is it not hard that a
person may have a soul as beautiful as an angel's, a
dwelling-place for all sweet sounds and harmonies,
and if nature has not thought fit to endow his body
with a chin the world will have none of him?
The vulgar prejudice is in favour of chins, and who
shall escape its influence? I, for one, cannot,
though theoretically I utterly reject the belief that
the body is the likeness of the soul; for has not
each of us friends who, we know, love beyond
everything that which is noble and good, and who
by no means themselves look noble and good?
And what about all the beautiful persons who love
nothing on earth except themselves? Yet who in
the world cares how perfect the nature may be, how
humble, how sweet, how gracious, that dwells in a
chinless body? Nobody has time to inquire into
natures, and the chinless must be content to be
treated in something of the same good-natured,
tolerant fashion in which we treat our poor relations
until such time as they shall have grown a beard;
and those who by their sex are for ever shut out
from this glorious possibility will have to take care,

should they be of a bright intelligence, how they speak with the tongues of men and of angels, nothing being more droll than the effect of high words and poetic ideas issuing from a face that does not match them.

I wish we were not so easily affected by each other's looks. Sometimes, during the course of a long correspondence with a friend, he grows to be inexpressibly dear to me ; I see how beautiful his soul is, how fine his intellect, how generous his heart, and how he already possesses in great perfection those qualities of kindness, and patience, and simplicity, after which I have been so long and so vainly striving. It is not I clothing him with the attributes I love and wandering away insensibly into that sweet land of illusions to which our footsteps turn whenever they are left to themselves, it is his very self unconsciously writing itself into his letters, the very man as he is without his body. Then I meet him again, and all illusions go. He is what I had always found him when we were together, good and amiable ; but some trick of manner, some feature or attitude that I do not quite like, makes me forget, and be totally unable to remember, what I know from his letters to be true of him. He, no doubt, feels the same thing about me, and so between us there is a thick veil of something fixed, which, dodge as we may, we never can get round.

"Well, and what do you conclude from all that?" said the Man of Wrath, who had been going out by the verandah door with his gun and his dogs to shoot the squirrels before they have eaten up too many birds, and of whose coat-sleeve I had laid hold as he passed, keeping him by me like a second Wedding Guest, and almost as restless, while I gave expression to the above sentiments.

"I don't know," I replied, "unless it is that the world is very evil and the times are waxing late, but that doesn't explain anything either, because it isn't true."

And he went down the steps laughing and shaking his head and muttering something that I could not quite catch, and I am glad I could not, for the two words I did hear were women and nonsense.

He has developed an unexpected passion for farming, much to my relief, and though we came down here at first only tentatively for a year, three have passed, and nothing has been said about going back to town. Nor will anything be said

so long as he is not the one to say it, for no three
years of my life can come up to these in happiness,
and not even those splendid years of childhood
that grow brighter as they recede were more full
of delights.   The delights are simple, it is true,
and of the sort that easily provoke a turning up of
the worldling's nose ; but who cares for noses that
turn up ?   I am simple myself, and never tire of
the blessed liberty from all restraints.   Even such
apparently indifferent details as being able to walk
straight out of doors without first getting into a
hat and gloves and veil are full of a subtle charm
that is ever fresh, and of which I can never have
too much.   It is clear that I was born for a placid
country life, and placid it certainly is ; so much so
that the days are sometimes far more like a dream
than anything real, the quiet days of reading, and
thinking, and watching the changing lights, and
the growth and fading of the flowers, the fresh
quiet days when life is so full of zest that you
cannot stop yourself from singing because you are
so happy, the warm quiet days lying on the grass
in a secluded corner observing the procession of
clouds—this being, I admit, a particularly undignified
attitude, but think of the edification !   Each morning the simple act of opening my bedroom windows

is the means of giving me an ever-recurring pleasure. Just underneath them is a border of rockets in full flower, at that hour in the shadow of the house, whose gables lie sharply defined on the grass beyond, and they send up their good morning of scent the moment they see me leaning out, careful not to omit the pretty German custom of morning greeting. I call back mine, embellished with many endearing words, and then their fragrance comes up close, and covers my face with gentlest little kisses. Behind them, on the other side of the lawn on this west side of the house, is a thick hedge of lilac just now at its best, and what that best is I wish all who love lilac could see. A century ago a man lived here who loved his garden. He loved, however, in his younger years, travelling as well, but in his travels did not forget this little corner of the earth belonging to him, and brought back the seeds of many strange trees such as had never been seen in these parts before, and tried experiments with them in the uncongenial soil, and though many perished a few took hold, and grew, and flourished, and shade me now at tea-time. What flowers he had, and how he arranged his beds, no one knows, except that the eleven beds round the sun-dial were put there by him ; and of

one thing he seems to have been inordinately fond,
and that was lilac. We have to thank him for the
surprising beauty of the garden in May and early
June, for he it was who planted the great groups
of it, and the banks of it, and massed it between
the pines and firs. Wherever a lilac bush could
go a lilac bush went ; and not common sorts, but
a variety of good sorts, white, and purple, and
pink, and mauve, and he must have planted it
with special care and discrimination, for it grows
here as nothing else will, and keeps his memory, in
my heart at least, for ever gratefully green. On
the wall behind our pew in church there is his
monument, he having died here full of years, in
the peace that attends the last hours of a good man
who has loved his garden ; and to the long Latin
praises of his virtues and eminence I add, as I pass
beneath it on Sundays, a heartiest Amen. Who
would not join in the praises of the man to whom
you owe your lilacs, and your Spanish chestnuts, and
your tulip trees, and your pyramid oaks? "He
was a good man, for he loved his garden"—that
is the epitaph I would have put on his monument,
because it gives one a far clearer sense of his
goodness and explains it better than any amount of
sonorous Latinities. How could he be anything *but*

good since he loved a garden—that divine filter that
filters all the grossness out of us, and leaves us,
each time we have been in it, clearer, and purer,
and more harmless?

June 16*th.*—Yesterday morning I got up at
three o'clock and stole through the echoing pass-
ages and strange dark rooms, undid with trembling
hands the bolts of the door to the verandah, and
passed out into a wonderful, unknown world. I
stood for a few minutes motionless on the steps,
almost frightened by the awful purity of nature
when all the sin and ugliness is shut up and asleep,
and there is nothing but the beauty left. It was
quite light, yet a bright moon hung in the cloudless grey-blue sky ; the flowers were all awake,
saturating the air with scent ; and a nightingale sat
on a hornbeam quite close to me, in loud raptures
at the coming of the sun. There in front of me
was the sun-dial, there were the rose bushes, there
was the bunch of pansies I had dropped the night
before still lying on the path, but how strange and
unfamiliar it all looked, and how holy—as though
God must be walking there in the cool of the day.
I went down the path leading to the stream on

the east side of the garden, brushing aside the
rockets that were bending across it drowsy with
dew, the larkspurs on either side of me rearing their
spikes of heavenly blue against the steely blue of
the sky, and the huge poppies like splashes of blood
amongst the greys and blues and faint pearly
whites of the innocent, new-born day. On the
garden side of the stream there is a long row of
silver birches, and on the other side a rye-field
reaching across in powdery grey waves to the part
of the sky where a solemn glow was already burning. I sat down on the twisted, half-fallen trunk
of a birch and waited, my feet in the long grass
and my slippers soaking in dew. Through the
trees I could see the house with its closed shutters
and drawn blinds, the people in it all missing, as I
have missed day after day, the beauty of life at
that hour. Just behind me the border of rockets
and larkspurs came to an end, and, turning my
head to watch a stealthy cat, my face brushed
against a wet truss of blossom and got its first
morning washing. It was wonderfully quiet, and
the nightingale on the hornbeam had everything to
itself as I sat motionless watching that glow in the
east burning redder ; wonderfully quiet, and so
wonderfully beautiful because one associates day-

light with people, and voices and bustle, and
hurryings to and fro, and the dreariness of working
to feed our bodies, and feeding our bodies that we
may be able to work to feed them again ; but here
was the world wide awake and yet only for me,
all the fresh pure air only for me, all the
fragrance breathed only by me, not a living
soul hearing the nightingale but me, the sun in a
few moments coming up to warm only me, and
nowhere a single hard word being spoken, or a
single selfish act being done, nowhere anything that
could tarnish the blessed purity of the world as
God has given it us. If one believed in angels one
would feel that they must love us best when we are
asleep and cannot hurt each other ; and what a
mercy it is that once in every twenty-four hours
we are too utterly weary to go on being unkind.
The doors shut, and the lights go out, and the
sharpest tongue is silent, and all of us, scolder and
scolded, happy and unhappy, master and slave,
judge and culprit, are children again, tired, and
hushed, and helpless, and forgiven. And see the
blessedness of sleep, that sends us back for a space
to our early innocence. Are not our first impulses
on waking always good? Do we not all know
how in times of wretchedness our first thoughts after

the night's sleep are happy? We have been dreaming we are happy, and we wake with a smile, and stare still smiling for a moment at our stony griefs before with a stab we recognise them.

There were no clouds, and presently, while I watched, the sun came up quickly out of the rye, a great, bare, red ball, and the grey of the field turned yellow, and long shadows lay upon the grass, and the wet flowers flashed out diamonds. And then as I sat there watching, and intensely happy as I imagined, suddenly the certainty of grief, and suffering, and death dropped like a black curtain between me and the beauty of the morning, and then that other thought, to face which needs all our courage— the realisation of the awful solitariness in which each of us lives and dies. Often I could cry for pity of our forlornness, and of the pathos of our endeavours to comfort ourselves. With what an agony of patience we build up the theories of consolation that are to protect, in times of trouble, our quivering and naked souls! And how fatally often the elaborate machinery refuses to work at the moment the blow is struck.

I got up and turned my face away from the un- bearable, indifferent brightness. Myriads of small

suns danced before my eyes as I went along the edge
of the stream to the seat round the oak in my spring
garden, where I sat a little, looking at the morning
from there, drinking it in in long breaths, and deter-
mining to think of nothing but just be happy.
What a smell of freshly mown grass there was,
and how the little heaps into which it had been
raked the evening before sparkled with dewdrops
as the sun caught them. And over there, how
hot the poppies were already beginning to look—
blazing back boldly in the face of the sun, flashing
back fire for fire. I crossed the wet grass to the
hammock under the beech on the lawn, and lay
in it a while trying to swing in time to the
nightingale's tune; and then I walked round
the ice-house to see how Goethe's corner looked
at such an hour; and then I went down to the
fir wood at the bottom of the garden where the
light was slanting through green stems; and
everywhere there was the same mystery, and
emptiness, and wonder. When four o'clock
drew near I set off home again, not desiring to
meet gardeners and have my little hour of quiet
talked about, still less my dressing-gown and
slippers; so I picked a bunch of roses and hurried
in, and just as I softly bolted the door, dreadfully

afraid of being taken for a burglar, I heard the first
water-cart of the day creaking round the corner.
Fearfully I crept up to my room, and when I awoke
at eight o'clock and saw the roses in a glass by
my side, I remembered what had happened as
though it had been years ago.

Now here I have had an experience that I shall
not soon forget, something very precious, and
private, and close to my soul ; a feeling as though
I had taken the world by surprise, and seen it as
it really is when off its guard—as though I had
been quite near to the very core of things.   The
quiet holiness of that hour seems all the more
mysterious now, because soon after breakfast
yesterday the wind began to blow from the north-
west, and has not left off since, and looking out
of the window I cannot believe that it is the
same garden, with the clouds driving over it in
black layers, and angry little showers every now
and then bespattering its harassed and helpless
inhabitants, who cannot pull their roots up out of
the ground and run for their lives, as I am sure
they must long to do.   How discouraging for a
plant to have just proudly opened its loveliest
flowers, the flowers it was dreaming about all the
winter and working at so busily underground

during the cold weeks of spring, and then for a
spiteful shower of five minutes' duration to come
and pelt them down, and batter them about, and
cover the tender, delicate things with irremediable
splashes of mud! Every bed is already filled with
victims of the gale, and those that escape one
shower go down before the next; so I must make
up my mind, I suppose, to the wholesale destruc-
tion of the flowers that had reached perfection—
that head of white rockets among them that
washed my face a hundred years ago—and look
forward cheerfully to the development of the
younger generation of buds which cannot yet
be harmed.

I know these gales. We get them quite
suddenly, always from the north-west, and always
cold. They ruin my garden for a day or
two, and in the summer try my temper, and at
all seasons try my skin; yet they are precious
because of the beautiful clear light they bring,
the intensity of cold blue in the sky and the
terrific purple blackness of the clouds one hour
and their divine whiteness the next. They fly
screaming over the plain as though ten thousand
devils with whips were after them, and in the sunny
intervals there is nothing in any of nature's moods

to equal the clear sharpness of the atmosphere, all
the mellowness and indistinctness beaten out of it,
and every leaf and twig glistening coldly bright.
It is not becoming, a north-westerly gale ; it treats
us as it treats the garden, but with opposite
results, roughly rubbing the softness out of our
faces, as I can see when I look at the babies, and
avoid the further proof of my own reflection in
the glass. But there is life in it, glowing, intense,
robust life, and when in October after weeks of
serene weather this gale suddenly pounces on us
in all its savageness, and the cold comes in a
gust, and the trees are stripped in an hour, what a
bracing feeling it is, the feeling that here is the first
breath of winter, that it is time to pull ourselves
together, that the season of work, and discipline,
and severity is upon us, the stern season that
forces us to look facts in the face, to put aside our
dreams and languors, and show what stuff we are
made of. No one can possibly love the summer,
the dear time of dreams, more passionately than
I do ; yet I have no desire to prolong it by
running off south when the winter approaches
and so cheat the year of half its lessons. It is
delightful and instructive to potter among one's
plants, but it is imperative for body and soul that

the pottering should cease for a few months, and
that we should be made to realise that grim other
side of life.   A long hard winter lived through from
beginning to end without shirking, is one of the
most salutary experiences in the world.   There
is no nonsense about it; you could not indulge
in vapours and the finer sentiments in the midst
of its deadly earnest if you tried.   The thermometer goes down to twenty degrees of frost
Réaumur, and down you go with it to the realities,
to that elementary state where everything is big—
health and sickness, delight and misery, ecstasy
and despair.   It makes you remember your poorer
neighbours, and sends you into their homes to see
that they too are fitted out with the armour of
warmth and food necessary in the long fight;
and in your own home it draws you nearer than
ever to each other.   Out of doors it is too cold
to walk, so you run, and are rewarded by the
conviction that you cannot be more than fifteen;
or you get into your furs, and dart away in a
sleigh over the snow, and are sure there never
was music so charming as that of its bells; or you
put on your skates, and are off to the lake to
which you drove so often on June nights, when it
lay rosy in the reflection of the northern glow,

and all alive with myriads of wild duck and plovers, and which is now, but for the swish of your skates, so silent, and but for your warmth and jollity, so forlorn. Nor would I willingly miss the early darkness and the pleasant firelight tea and the long evenings among my books. It is then that I am glad I do not live in a cave, as I confess I have in my more godlike moments wished to do ; it is then that I feel most capable of attending to the Man of Wrath's exhortations with an open mind ; it is then that I actually like to hear the shrieks of the wind, and then that I give my heartiest assent, as I warm my feet at the fire, to the poet's proposition that all which we behold is full of blessings.

But what dreariness can equal the dreariness of a cold gale at midsummer? I have been chilly and dejected all day, shut up behind the streaming window-panes, and not liking to have a fire because of its dissipated appearance in the scorching intervals of sunshine. Once or twice my hand was on the bell and I was going to order one, when out came the sun and it was June again, and I ran joyfully into the dripping, gleaming garden, only to be driven in five minutes later by a yet fiercer squall. I wandered disconsolately round my pillar of books, looking for the one that would lend itself best to the task of entertaining me under the prevailing conditions, but they all looked gloomy, and reserved, and forbidding. So I sat down in a very big chair, and reflected that if there were to be many days like this it might be as well to ask somebody cheerful to come and sit opposite me in all those other big chairs that were looking so unusually gigantic and empty. When the Man of Wrath came in to tea there were such heavy clouds that the room was quite dark, and he peered about for a moment before he saw me. I suppose in the gloom of the big room I must have looked rather lonely, and smaller than usual buried in the capacious chair, for when he finally discovered me his face widened into an inappropriately cheerful smile.

" Well, my dear," he said genially, " how very cold it is."

" Did you come in to say that? " I asked.

" This tempest is very unusual in the summer," he proceeded ; to which I made no reply of any sort

" I did not see you at first amongst all these chairs and cushions. At least, I saw you, but it is so dark I thought you were a cushion."

Now no woman likes to be taken for a cushion, so I rose and began to make tea with an icy dignity of demeanour.

"I am afraid I shall be forced to break my promise not to invite any one here," he said, watching my face as he spoke. My heart gave a distinct leap—so small is the constancy and fortitude of woman. "But it will only be for one night." My heart sank down as though it were lead. "And I have just received a telegram that it will be to-night." Up went my heart with a cheerful bound.

"Who is it?" I inquired. And then he told me that it was the least objectionable of the candidates for the living here, made vacant by our own parson having been appointed superintendent, the highest position in the Lutheran Church; and the gale must have brought me low indeed for the coming of a solitary parson to give me pleasure. The entire race of Lutheran parsons is unpleasing to me—whether owing to their fault or to mine, it would ill become me to say,—and the one we are losing is the only one I have met that I can heartily respect, and admire, and like. But he is quite one by himself in his extreme godliness, perfect simplicity, and real humility, and though

I knew it was unlikely we should find another as good, and I despised myself for the eagerness with which I felt I was looking forward to seeing a new face, I could not stop myself from suddenly feeling cheerful. Such is the weakness of the female mind, and such the unexpected consequences of two months' complete solitude with forty-eight hours' gale at the end of them.

We have had countless applications during the last few weeks for the living, as it is a specially fat one for this part of the country, with a yearly income of six thousand marks, and a good house, and several acres of land. The Man of Wrath has been distracted by the difficulties of choice. According to the letters of recommendation, they were all wonderful men with unrivalled powers of preaching, but on closer inquiry there was sure to be some drawback. One was too old, another not old enough ; another had twelve children, and the parsonage only allows for eight ; one had a shrewish wife, and another was of Liberal tendencies in politics—a fatal objection ; one was in money difficulties because he would spend more than he had, which was not surprising when one heard what he did have ; and another was disliked in his parish because he and his wife were too close-fisted and would not spend at all ; and at last, the Man of Wrath explained, the moment having arrived when if he did not himself appoint somebody his right to do so would lapse, he had written to the one who was coming, and invited him down that he might look at him, and ask him searching questions as to the faith which is in him.

I forgot my gloom, and my half-formed desperate resolve to break my vow of solitude and fill the house with the frivolous, as I sat listening to the cheerful talk of the little parson this evening. He was so cheerful, yet it was hard to see any cause for it in the life he was leading, a life led by the great majority of the German clergy, fat livings being as rare here as anywhere else. He told us with pleasant frankness all about himself, how he lived on an income of two thousand marks with a wife and six children, and how he was often sorely put to it to keep decent shoes on their feet. " I am continually drawing up plans of expenditure," he said, " but the shoemaker's bill is always so much more than I had expected that it throws my calculations completely out."

His wife, of course, was ailing, but already his eldest child, a girl of ten, took a great deal of the work off her mother's shoulders, poor baby. He

was perfectly natural, and said in the simplest way
that if the choice were to fall on him it would
relieve him of many grinding anxieties; whereupon I privately determined that if the choice did
not fall on him the Man of Wrath and I would
be strangers from that hour.

"Have you been worrying him with questions
about his principles?" I asked, buttonholing the
Man of Wrath as he came out from a private
conference with him.

"Principles? My dear Elizabeth, how can he
have any on that income?"

"If he is not a Conservative will you let that
stand in his way, and doom that little child to
go on taking work off other people's shoulders?"

"My dear Elizabeth," he protested, "what
has my decision for or against him to do with
dooming little children to go on doing anything? I really cannot be governed by senti-
ment."

"If you don't give it to him—" and I held
up an awful finger of warning as he retreated, at
which he only laughed.

When the parson came to say good-night and
good-bye, as he was leaving very early in the morning, I saw at once by his face that all was right.

He bent over my hand, stammering out words of thanks and promises of devotion and invocations of blessings in such quantities that I began to feel quite pleased with myself, and as though I had been doing a virtuous deed. This feeling I saw reflected on the Man of Wrath's face, which made me consider that all we had done was to fill the living in the way that suited us best, and that we had no cause whatever to look and feel so benevolent. Still, even now, while the victorious candidate is dreaming of his trebled income and of the raptures of his home-coming to-morrow, the glow has not quite departed, and I am dwelling with satisfaction on the fact that we have been able to raise eight people above those hideous cares that crush all the colour out of the lives of the genteel poor. I am glad he has so many children, because there will be more to be made happy. They will be rich on the little income, and will no doubt dismiss the wise and willing eldest baby to appropriate dolls and pinafores ; and everybody will have what they never yet have had, a certain amount of that priceless boon, leisure—leisure to sit down and look at themselves, and inquire what it is they really mean, and really want, and really intend to do with their lives. And this, I may observe, is a beneficial process wholly impossible on £100 a year divided by eight.

But I wonder whether they will be thin-skinned enough ever to discover that other and less delightful side of life only seen by those who have plenty of leisure. Sordid cares may be very terrible to the sensitive, and make them miss the best of everything, but as long as they have them and are busy from morning till night keeping up appearances, they miss also the burden of those fears, and dreads, and realisations that beset him who has time to think. When in the morning I go into my sausage-room and give out sausages, I never think of anything but sausages. My horizon is bounded by them, every faculty is absorbed by them, and they engross me, while I am with them, to the exclusion of the whole world. Not that I love them ; as far as that goes, unlike the effect they produce on most of my country-men, they leave me singularly cold ; but it is one of my duties to begin the day with sausages, and every morning for the short time I am in the midst of their shining rows, watching my *Mamsell* dexterously hooking down the sleekest with an instrument like a boat-hook, I am practically dead to every other consideration in heaven or on earth.

What are they to me, Love, Life, Death, all the mysteries? The one thing that concerns me is the due distribution to the servants of sausages; and until that is done, all obstinate questionings and blank misgivings must wait. If I were to spend my days in their entirety doing such work I should never have time to think, and if I never thought I should never feel, and if I never felt I should never suffer or rapturously enjoy, and so I should grow to be something very like a sausage myself, and not on that account, I do believe, any the less precious to the Man of Wrath.

I know what I would do if I were both poor and genteel—the gentility should go to the place of all good ilities, including utility, respectability, and imbecility, and I would sit, quite frankly poor, with a piece of bread, and a pot of geraniums, and a book. I conclude that if I did without the things erroneously supposed necessary to decency I might be able to afford a geranium, because I see them so often in the windows of cottages where there is little else; and if I preferred such inexpensive indulgences as thinking and reading and wandering in the fields to the doubtful gratification arising from kept-up appearances (always for the bedazzlement of the people opposite, and therefore always vulgar), I believe I should have enough left over to buy a radish to eat with my bread ; and if the weather were fine, and I could eat it under a tree, and give a robin some crumbs in return for his cheeriness, would there be another creature in the world so happy? I know there would not.

July

JULY

July 1*st.*—I think that after roses sweet-peas are my favourite flowers. Nobody, except the ultra-original, denies the absolute supremacy of the rose. She is safe on her throne, and the only question to decide is which are the flowers that one loves next best. This I have been a long while deciding, though I believe I knew all the time somewhere deep down in my heart that they were sweet-peas; and every summer when they first come out, and every time, going round the garden, that I come across them, I murmur involuntarily, "Oh yes, *you* are the sweetest, you dear, dear little things." And what a victory this is, to be ranked next the rose even by one person who loves her garden. Think of the wonderful beauty triumphed over—the lilies,

the irises, the carnations, the violets, the frail and
delicate poppies, the magnificent larkspurs, the
burning nasturtiums, the fierce marigolds, the
smooth, cool pansies. I have a bed at this
moment in the full glory of all these things, a
little chosen plot of fertile land, about fifteen
yards long and of irregular breadth, shutting in
at its broadest the east end of the walk along the
south front of the house, and sloping away at the
back down to a moist, low bit by the side of a
very tiny stream, or rather thread of trickling
water, where, in the dampest corner, shining in
the sun, but with their feet kept cool and wet, is a
colony of Japanese irises, and next to them higher
on the slope Madonna lilies, so chaste in looks
and so voluptuous in smell, and then a group of
hollyhocks in tenderest shades of pink, and lemon,
and white, and right and left of these white
marguerites and evening primroses and that most
exquisite of poppies called Shirley, and a little on
one side a group of metallic blue delphiniums
beside a towering white lupin, and in and out
and everywhere mignonette, and stocks, and pinks,
and a dozen other smaller but not less lovely
plants. I wish I were a poet, that I might properly
describe the beauty of this bit as it sparkles this

afternoon in the sunshine after rain ; but of all the charming, delicate, scented groups it contains, none to my mind is so lovely as the group of sweet-peas in its north-west corner. There is something so utterly gentle and tender about sweet-peas, something so endearing in their clinging, winding, yielding growth ; and then the long straight stalk, and the perfect little winged flower at the top, with its soft, pearly texture and wonderful range and combination of colours—all of them pure, all of them satisfying, not an ugly one, or even a less beautiful one among them. And in the house, next to a china bowl of roses, there is no arrangement of flowers so lovely as a bowl of sweet-peas, or a Delf jar filled with them. What a mass of glowing, yet delicate colour it is ! How prettily, the moment you open the door, it seems to send its fragrance to meet you ! And how you hang over it, and bury your face in it, and love it, and cannot get away from it. I really am sorry for all the people in the world who miss such keen pleasure. It is one that each person who opens his eyes and his heart may have ; and indeed, most of the things that are really worth having are within everybody's reach. Any one who chooses to take a country walk, or even the small amount of trouble necessary to get him on to his doorstep and make him open his eyes, may have them, and there are thousands of them thrust upon us by nature, who is for ever giving and blessing, at every turn as we walk. The sight of the first pale flowers starring the copses ; an anemone held up against the blue sky with the sun shining through it towards you ; the first fall of snow in the autumn ; the first thaw of snow in the spring ; the blustering, busy winds blowing the winter away and scurrying the dead, untidy leaves into the corners ; the hot smell of pines— just like blackberries—when the sun is on them ; the first February evening that is fine enough to show how the days are lengthening, with its pale yellow strip of sky behind the black trees whose branches are pearled with raindrops ; the swift pang of realisation that the winter is gone and the spring is coming ; the smell of the young larches a few weeks later ; the bunch of cow-slips that you kiss and kiss again because it is so perfect, because it is so divinely sweet, because of all the kisses in the world there is none other so exquisite—who that has felt the joy of these things would exchange them, even if in return he were to gain the whole world, with all its chimney-

pots, and bricks, and dust, and dreariness? And
we know that the gain of a world never yet made
up for the loss of a soul.

One day, in going round the head inspector's
garden with his wife, whose care it is, I remarked with surprise that she had no sweet-peas.
I called them *Lathyrus odoratus*, and she, having
little Latin, did not understand. Then I called
them *wohlriechende Wicken*, the German render-
ing of that which sounds so pretty in English,
and she said she had never heard of them.
The idea of an existence in a garden yet without sweet-peas, so willing, so modest, and so
easily grown, had never presented itself as possible to my imagination. Ever since I can
remember, my summers have been filled with
them; and in the days when I sat in my own
perambulator and they were three times as tall as
I was, I well recollect a certain waving hedge of
them in the garden of my childhood and how I
stared up longingly at the flowers so far beyond
my reach, inaccessibly tossing against the sky.
When I grew bigger and had a small garden of
my own, I bought their seeds to the extent of
twenty pfennings, and trained the plants over the
rabbit-hutch that was the chief feature in the

landscape. There were other seeds in that garden, seeds on which I had laid out all my savings and round which played my fondest hopes, but the sweet-peas were the only ones that came up. The same thing happened here in my first summer, my gardening knowledge not having meanwhile kept pace with my years, and of the seeds sown that first season sweet-peas again were the only ones that came up. I should say they were just the things for people with very little time and experience at their disposal to grow. A garden might be made beautiful with sweet-peas alone, and, with hardly any labour, except the sweet labour of picking to prolong the bloom, be turned into a fairy bower of delicacy and refinement. Yet the Frau Inspector not only had never heard of them, but, on my showing her a bunch, was not in the least impressed, and led me in her garden to a number of those exceedingly vulgar red herbaceous peonies growing among her currant bushes, and announced with conviction that they were her favourite flower. It was on the tip of my tongue to point out that in these days of tree-peonies, and peonies so lovely in their silvery faint tints that they resemble gigantic roses, it is absolutely wicked to suffer those odious red ones to pervert one's taste; that a person who sees nothing but those every time he looks out of his window very quickly has his nice perception for true beauty blunted; that such a person would do well to visit my garden every day during the month of May, and so get himself cured by the sight of my peony bushes covered with huge scented white and blush flowers; and that he would, I was convinced, at the end of the cure, go home and pitch his own on to the dust-heap. But of what earthly use would it have been? Pointing out the difference between what is beautiful and what misses beauty to a Frau Inspector of forty, whose chief business it is to make butter, is likely to be singularly unprolific of good results; and, further, experience has taught me that whenever anything is on the tip of my tongue the best thing to do is to keep it there. I wonder why a woman always wants to interfere.

It is a pity, nevertheless, that this lady should be so wanting in the æsthetic instinct, for her garden is full of possibilities. It lies due south, sheltered on the north, east, and west by farm buildings, and is rich in those old fruit-trees and well-seasoned gooseberry bushes that make such a good basis for the formation of that most delightful type of little garden, the flower-and-fruit-and vegetable-mixed sort. She has, besides, an inestimable slimy, froggy pond, a perpetual treasure of malodorous water, much pined after by thirsty flowers ; and then does she not live in the middle of a farmyard flowing with fertilising properties that only require a bucket and a shovel to transform them into roses ? The way in which people miss their opportunities is melancholy.

This pond of hers, by the way, is an object of the liveliest interest to the babies. They do not seem to mind the smell, and they love the slime, and they had played there for several days in great peace before the unfortunate accident of the June baby's falling in and being brought back looking like a green and speckled frog herself, revealed where it was they had persuaded Séraphine to let them spend their mornings. Then there was woe and lamentation, for I was sure they would all have typhoid fever, and I put them mercilessly to bed, and dosed them, as a preliminary, with castor oil—that oil of sorrow, as Carlyle calls it. It was no use sending for the doctor because there is no doctor within reach ; a fact which simplifies life amazingly when you have children. During the time we lived in town the doctor was never out of

the house. Hardly a day passed but one or other
of the Three had a spot, or, as the expressive
German has it, a *Pickel*, and what parent could
resist sending for a doctor when one lived round
the corner ? But doctors are like bad habits—
once you have shaken them off you discover how
much better you are without them ; and as for
the babies, since they inhabit a garden, prompt
bed and the above-mentioned simple remedy
have been all that is necessary to keep them
robust. I admit I was frightened when I heard
where they had been playing, for when the wind
comes from that quarter even sitting by my rose beds
I have been reminded of the existence of the pond ;
and I kept them in bed for three days, anxiously
awaiting symptoms, and my head full of a dreadful
story I had heard of a little boy who had drunk
seltzer water and thereupon been seized with
typhoid fever and had died, and if, I asked myself
with a power of reasoning unusual in a woman,
you die after seltzer water, what will you not do
after frog-pond ? But they did nothing, except
be uproarious, and sing at the top of their voices,
and clamour for more dinner than I felt would be
appropriate for babies who were going to be
dangerously ill in a few hours ; and so, after due

waiting, they were got up and dressed and turned loose again, and from that day to this no symptoms have appeared. The pond was at first strictly forbidden as a playground, but afterwards I made concessions, and now they are allowed to go to a deserted little burying-ground on the west side of it when the wind is in the west ; and there at least they can hear the frogs, and sometimes, if they are patient, catch a delightful glimpse of them.

The graveyard is in the middle of a group of pines that bounds the Frau Inspector's garden on that side, and has not been used within the memory of living man. The people here love to make their little burying-grounds in the heart of a wood if they can, and they are often a long way away from the church to which they belong because, while every hamlet has its burying-ground, three or four hamlets have to share a church ; and indeed the need for churches is not so urgent as that for graves, seeing that, though we may not all go to church, we all of us die and must be buried. Some of these little cemeteries are not even anywhere near a village, and you come upon them unexpectedly in your drives through the woods — bits of fenced-in forest, the old gates dropping off their hinges, the paths green from long disuse, the unchecked trees casting black, impenetrable shadows across the poor, meek, pathetic graves. I try sometimes, pushing aside the weeds, to decipher the legend on the almost speechless headstones; but the voice has been choked out of them by years of wind, and frost, and snow, and a few stray letters are all that they can utter—a last stammering protest against oblivion.

The Man of Wrath says all women love churchyards. He is fond of sweeping assertions, and is sometimes curiously feminine in his tendency to infer a general principle from a particular instance. The deserted little forest burying-grounds interest and touch me because they are so solitary, and humble, and neglected, and forgotten, and because so many long years have passed since tears were shed over the newly-made graves. Nobody cries now for the husband, or father, or brother buried there; years and years ago the last tear that would ever be shed for them was dried—dried probably before the gate was reached on the way home—and they were not missed. Love and sorrow appear to be flowers of civilisation, and most to flourish where life has the broadest margin of leisure and abundance. The

primary instincts are always there, and must first
be satisfied ; and if to obtain the means of satisfying them you have to work from morning till
night without rest, who shall find time and energy
to sit down and lament ?   I often go with the babies
to the enclosure near the Frau Inspector's pond, and
it seems just as natural that they should play there
as that the white butterflies should chase each
other undisturbed across the shadows.   And then
the place has a soothing influence on them, and
they sober down as we approach it, and on hot
afternoons sit quietly enough as close to the pond
as they may, content to watch for the chance
appearance of a frog while talking to me about
angels.

This is their favourite topic of conversation in this particular place.   Just as I have
special times and places for certain books, so do
they seem to have special times and places for
certain talk.   The first time I took them there
they asked me what the mounds were, and by a
series of adroit questions extracted the information that the people who had been buried there
were now angels (I am not a specialist, and must
take refuge in telling them what I was told in my
youth), and ever since then they refuse to call it a

graveyard, and have christened it the angel-yard, and so have got into the way of discussing angels in all their bearings, sometimes to my confusion, whenever we go there.

" But what *are* angels, mummy ? " said the June baby inconsequently this afternoon, after having assisted at the discussions for several days and apparently listening with attention.

" *Such* a silly baby ! " cried April, turning upon her with contempt, " don't you know they are *lieber Gott's* little girls ? "

Now I protest I had never told those babies anything of the sort. I answer their questions to the best of my ability and as conscientiously as I can, and then, when I hear them talking together afterwards, I am staggered by the impression they appear to have received. They live in a whole world of independent ideas in regard to heaven and the angels, ideas quite distinct from other people's, and, as far as I can make out, believe that the Being they call *lieber Gott* pervades the garden, and is identical with, among other things, the sunshine and the air on a fine day. I never told them so, nor, I am sure, did Séraphine, and still less Séraphine's predecessor Miss Jones, whose views were wholly material ; yet if, on bright

mornings, I forget to immediately open all the
library windows on coming down, the April baby
runs in, and with quite a worried look on her face
cries, "Mummy, won't you open the windows and
let the *lieber Gott* come in ?"

If they were less rosy and hungry, or if I were
less prosaic, I might have gloomy forebodings that
such keen interest in things and beings celestial
was prophetic of a short life ; and in books, we
know, the children who talk much on these topics
invariably die, after having given their reverential
parents a quantity of advice. Fortunately such
children are confined to books, and there is
nothing of the ministering child—surely a very
uncomfortable form of infant—about my babies.
Indeed, I notice that in their conversations together
on such matters a healthy spirit of contradiction
prevails, and this afternoon, after having accepted
April's definition of angels with apparent rever-
ence, the June baby electrified the other two
(always more orthodox and yielding) by remarking that she hoped she would never go to heaven.
I pretended to be deep in my book and not
listening ; April and May were sitting on the
grass sewing ("needling" they call it) fearful-look-
ing woolwork things for Séraphine's birthday,

and June was leaning idly against a pine trunk, swinging a headless doll round and round by its one remaining leg, her heels well dug into the ground, her sun-bonnet off, and all the yellow tangles of her hair falling across her sunburnt, grimy little face.

"No," she repeated firmly, with her eyes fixed on her sisters' startled faces, "I don't want to. There's nothing there for babies to play with."

"Nothing to play with?" exclaimed the other two in a breath—and throwing down their needle-work they made a simultaneous rush for me.

"Mummy, did you hear? June says she doesn't want to go into the *Himmel!*" cried April, horror-stricken.

"Because there's nothing to play with there, she says," cried May breathlessly; and then they added with one voice, as though the subject had long ago been threshed out and settled between them, "Why, she can play at ball there with all the *Sternleins* if she likes!"

The idea of the June baby striding across the firmament and hurling the stars about as carelessly as though they were tennis-balls was so magnificent that it sent shivers of awe through me as I read.

"But if you break all your dolls," added April,

turning severely to June, and eyeing the distorted remains in her hand, "I don't think *lieber Gott* will let you in at all. When you're big and have tiny Junes—real live Junes—I think you'll break them too, and *lieber Gott* doesn't love mummies what breaks their babies."

"But I *must* break my dolls," cried June, stung into indignation by what she evidently regarded as celestial injustice ; "*lieber Gott* made me that way, so I can't help doing it, can I, mummy ?"

On these occasions I keep my eyes fixed on my book, and put on an air of deep abstraction ; and indeed, it is the only way of keeping out of theological disputes in which I am invariably worsted.

July 15*th.*—Yesterday, as it was a cool and windy afternoon and not as pleasant in my garden as it has lately been, I thought I would go into the village and see how my friends the farm hands were getting on. Philanthropy is intermittent with me as with most people, only they do not say so, and seizes me like a cold in the head whenever the weather is chilly. On warm days my bump of

benevolence melts away entirely, and grows bigger in
proportion as the thermometer descends. When
the wind is in the east it is quite a decent size, and
about January, in a north-easterly snowstorm, it is
plainly visible to the most casual observer. For a
few weeks from then to the end of February I can
hold up my head and look our parson in the face,
but during the summer, if I see him coming my mode
of progression in getting out of the way is described
with perfect accuracy by the verb " to slink."

The village consists of one street running
parallel to the outer buildings of the farm, and
the cottages are one-storied, each with rooms for
four families—two in front, looking on to the wall
of the farmyard, which is the fashionable side, and
two at the back, looking on to nothing more
exhilarating than their own pigstyes. Each family
has one room and a larder sort of place, and shares
the kitchen with the family on the opposite side of
the entrance ; but the women prefer doing their
cooking at the grate in their own room rather
than expose the contents of their pots to the ill-
natured comments of a neighbour. On the
fashionable side there is a little fenced-in garden
for every family, where fowls walk about pensively
and meditate beneath the scarlet-runners (for all

the world like me in my garden), and hollyhocks tower above the drying linen, and fuel, stolen from our woods, is stacked for winter use; but on the other side you walk straight out of the door on to manure heaps and pigs.

The street did not look very inviting yesterday, with a lowering sky above, and the wind blowing dust and bits of straw and paper into my face and preventing me from seeing what I knew to be there, a consoling glimpse of green fields and fir woods down at the other end; but I had not been for a long while—we have had such a lovely summer—and something inside me had kept on saying aggressively all the morning, "Elizabeth, don't you know you are due in the village? Why don't you go then? When are you going? Don't you know you *ought* to go? Don't you feel you *must?* Elizabeth, pull yourself together and *go*." Strange effect of a grey sky and a cool wind! For I protest that if it had been warm and sunny my conscience would not have bothered about me at all. We had a short fight over it, in which I got all the knocks, as was evident by the immediate swelling of the bump alluded to above, and then I gave in, and by two o'clock in the afternoon was lifting the latch of the first door and asking the woman who lived behind it what she had given the family for dinner. This, I was instructed on my first round by the Frau Inspector, is the proper thing to ask ; and if you can follow it up by an examination of the contents of the saucepan, and a gentle sniff indicative of your appreciation of their savouriness, so much the better. I was diffident at first about this, but the gratification on their faces at the interest displayed is so unmistakable that I never now omit going through the whole business. This woman, the wife of one of the men who clean and feed the cows, has arrived at that enviable stage of exist-ence when her children have all been confirmed and can go out to work, leaving her to spend her days in her clean and empty room in comparative dignity and peace. The children go to school till they are fourteen, then they are confirmed, are considered grown up, and begin to work for wages ; and her three strapping daughters were out in the fields yesterday reaping. The mother has a keen, shrewd face, and everything about her was neat and comfortable. Her floor was freshly strewn with sand, her cups and saucers and spoons shone bright and clean from behind the glass door of the cupboard, and the two beds, one for herself and her husband and the other for her three daughters, were more mountainous than any I afterwards saw. The size and plumpness of her feather beds, the Frau Inspector tells me, is a woman's chief claim to consideration from the neighbours. She who can pile them up nearest to the ceiling becomes the principal personage in the community, and a flat bed is a social disgrace. It is a mystery to me, when I see the narrowness of the bedsteads, how so many people can sleep in them. They are rather narrower than what are known as single beds, yet father and mother and often a baby manage to sleep very well in one, and three or four children in the opposite corner of the room in another. The explanation no doubt is that they do not know what nerves are, and what it is to be wakened by the slightest sound or movement in the room and lie for hours afterwards, often the whole night, totally unable to fall asleep again, staring out into the darkness with eyes that refuse to shut. No nerves, and a thick skin—what inestimable blessings to these poor people! And they never heard of either.

I stood a little while talking, not asked to sit down, for that would be thought a liberty, and hearing how they had had potatoes and bacon for dinner, and how the eldest girl Bertha was going to be married at Michaelmas, and how well her baby was getting through its teething.

" Her baby ? " I echoed, " I have not heard of a baby ? "

The woman went to one of the beds and lifted up a corner of the great bag of feathers, and there, sure enough, lay a round and placid baby, sleeping as sweetly and looking as cherubic as the most legitimate of its contemporaries.

"And he is going to marry her at Michaelmas ? " I asked, looking as sternly as I could at the grandmother.

"Oh yes," she replied, " he is a good young man, and earns eighteen marks a week. They will be very comfortable."

"It is a pity," I said, "that the baby did not make its appearance after Michaelmas instead of before. Don't you see yourself what a pity it is, and how everything has been spoilt ? "

She stared at me for a moment with a puzzled look, and then turned away and carefully covered the cherub again. "They will be very comfortable," she repeated, seeing that I expected an answer ; " he earns eighteen marks a week."

What was there to be said ? If I had told her

her daughter was a grievous sinner she might perhaps have felt transiently uncomfortable, but as soon as I had gone would have seen for herself, with those shrewd eyes of hers, that nothing had been changed by my denunciations, that there lay the baby, dimpled and healthy, that her daughter was making a good match, that none of her set saw anything amiss, and that all the young couples in the district had prefaced their marriages in this way.

Our parson is troubled to the depths of his sensitive soul by this custom. He preaches, he expostulates, he denounces, he implores, and they listen with square stolid faces and open mouths, and go back to their daily work among their friends and acquaintances, with no feeling of shame, because everybody does it, and public opinion, the only force that could stop it, is on their side. The parson looks on with unutterable sadness at the futility of his efforts; but the material is altogether too raw for successful manipulation by delicate fingers.

"Poor things," I said one day, in answer to an outburst of indignation from him, after he had been marrying one of our servants at the eleventh hour, "I am so sorry for them. It is so pitiful that they should always have to be scolded on their wedding day. Such children—so ignorant, so uncontrolled, so frankly animal—what do they know about social laws ? They only know and follow nature, and I would from my heart forgive them all."

"It is *sin*," he said shortly.

"Then the forgiveness is sure."

"Not if they do not seek it."

I was silent, for I wished to reply that I believed they would be forgiven in spite of themselves, that probably they were forgiven whether they sought it or not, and that you cannot limit things divine ; but who can argue with a parson? These people do not seek forgiveness because it never enters their heads that they need it. The parson tells them so, it is true, but they regard him as a person bound by his profession to say that sort of thing, and are sharp enough to see that the consequences of their sin, foretold by him with such awful eloquence, never by any chance come off. No girl is left to languish and die forsaken by her betrayer, for the betrayer is a worthy young man who marries her as soon as he possibly can ; no finger of scorn is pointed at the fallen one, for all the fingers in the street are attached to women who began life in precisely the same fashion ; and as for that problematical Day of Judgment of which they hear so much on Sundays, perhaps they feel that that also may be one of the things which after all do not happen.

The servant who had been married and scolded that morning was a groom, aged twenty, and he had met his little wife, she being then seventeen, in the place he was in before he came to us. She was a housemaid there, and must have been a pretty thing, though there were few enough traces of it, except the beautiful eyes, in the little anxious face that I saw for the first time immediately after the wedding, and just before the weary and harassed parson came in to talk things over. I had never heard of her existence until, about ten days previously, the groom had appeared, bathed in tears, speechlessly holding out a letter from her in which she said she could not bear things any longer and was going to kill herself. The wretched young man was at his wits' end, for he had not yet saved enough to buy any furniture and set up housekeeping, and she was penniless after so many months out of a situation. He did not know any way out of it, he had no suggestions to offer, no excuses to make, and just stood there helplessly and sobbed.

I went to the Man of Wrath, and we laid our heads together. "We do not want another married servant," he said.

"No, of course we don't," said I.

"And there is not a room empty in the village."

"No, not one."

"And how can we give him furniture? It is not fair to the other servants who remain virtuous, and wait till they can buy their own."

"No, certainly it isn't fair."

There was a pause.

"He is a good boy," I murmured presently.

"A very good boy."

"And she will be quite ruined unless somebody——"

"I'll tell you what we can do, Elizabeth," he interrupted; "we can buy what is needful and let him have it on condition that he buys it back gradually by some small monthly payment."

"So we can."

"And I think there is a room over the stables that is empty."

"So there is."

"And he can go to town and get what furniture he needs and bring the girl back with him and marry her at once. The sooner the better, poor girl."

And so within a fortnight they were married, and came hand in hand to me, he proud and happy, holding himself very straight, she in no wise yet recovered from the shock and misery of the last few hopeless months, looking up at me with eyes grown much too big for her face, eyes in which there still lurked the frightened look caught in the town where she had hidden herself, and where fingers of scorn could not have been wanting, and loud derision, and utter shame, besides the burden of sickness, and hunger, and miserable pitiful youth.

They stood hand in hand, she in a decent black dress, and both wearing very tight white kid gloves that refused to hide entirely the whole of the rough red hands, and they looked so ridiculously young, and the whole thing was so wildly improvident, that no words of exhortation would come to my lips as I gazed at them in silence, between laughter and tears. I ought to have told them they were sinners ; I ought to have told them they were reckless ; I ought to have told them by what a narrow chance they had escaped the just punishment of their iniquity, and instead of that I found myself stretching out hands that were at once seized and kissed, and merely saying with a cheerful smile,

" *Nun Kinder, liebt Euch, und seid brav.*"   And
so they were dismissed, and then the parson came,
in a fever at this latest example of deadly sin, while
I, with the want of moral sense so often observable
in woman, could only think with pity of their
childishness.   The baby was born three days later,
and the mother very nearly slipped through our
fingers ; but she was a country girl, and she fought
round, and by and by grew young again in the
warmth of married respectability ; and I met her
the other day airing her baby in the sun, and
holding her head as high as though she were
conscious of a whole row of feather beds at home,
every one of which touched the ceiling.

In the next room I went into an old woman
lay in bed with her head tied up in bandages.
The room had not much in it, or it would have
been untidier ; it looked neglected and gloomy,
and some dirty plates, suggestive of long-past
dinners, were piled on the table.

" Oh, such headaches ! " groaned the old woman
when she saw me, and moved her head from side
to side on the pillow.   I could see she was not
undressed, and had crept under her feather bag as
she was.   I went to the bedside and felt her pulse
—a steady pulse, with nothing of feverishness in it.

"Oh, such draughts!" moaned the old woman, when she saw I had left the door open.

"A little air will make you feel better," I said ; the atmosphere in the shut-up room was so indescribable that my own head had begun to throb.

"Oh, oh!" she moaned, in visible indignation at being forced for a moment to breathe the pure summer air.

"I have something at home that will cure your headache," I said, "but there is nobody I can send with it to-day. If you feel better later on, come round and fetch it. I always take it when I have a headache"—("Why, Elizabeth, you know you never have such things!" whispered my conscience, appalled. "You just keep quiet," I whispered back, "I have had enough of you for one day.")—"and I have some grapes I will give you when you come, so that if you possibly can, do."

"Oh, I can't move," groaned the old woman, "oh, oh, oh!" But I went away laughing, for I knew she would appear punctually to fetch the grapes, and a walk in the air was all she needed to cure her.

How the whole village hates and dreads fresh air! A baby died a few days ago, killed, I

honestly believe, by the exceeding love of its
mother, which took the form of cherishing it so
tenderly that never once during its little life was
a breath of air allowed to come anywhere near it.
She is the watchman's wife, a gentle, flabby woman,
with two rooms at her disposal, but preferring to
live and sleep with her four children in one, never
going into the other except for the christenings
and funerals which take place in her family with
what I cannot but regard as unnecessary frequency.
This baby was born last September in a time of
golden days and quiet skies, and when it was
about three weeks old I suggested that she should
take it out every day while the fine weather lasted.
She pointed out that it had not yet been christened,
and remembering that it is the custom in their
class for both mother and child to remain shut up
and invisible till after the christening, I said no
more. Three weeks later I was its godmother,
and it was safely got into the fold of the Church.
As I was leaving, I remarked that now she would
be able to take it out as much as she liked. The
following March, on a day that smelt of violets,
I met her near the house. I asked after the baby,
and she began to cry. "It does not thrive," she
wept, "and its arms are no thicker than my finger."

"Keep it out in the sun as much as you can," I said; "this is the very weather to turn weak babies into strong ones."

"Oh, I am so afraid it will catch cold if I take it out," she cried, her face buried in what was once a pocket handkerchief.

"When was it out last?"

"Oh——" she stopped to blow her nose, very violently, and, as it seemed to me, with superfluous thoroughness. I waited till she had done, and then repeated my question.

"Oh——" a fresh burst of tears, and renewed exhaustive nose-blowing.

I began to suspect that my question, put casually, was of more importance than I had thought, and repeated it once more.

"I—can't t—take it out," she sobbed, "I know it—it would die."

"But has it not been out at all, then?"

She shook her head.

"Not once since it was born? Six months ago?"

She shook her head.

"*Poor* baby!" I exclaimed; and indeed from my heart I pitied the little thing, perishing in a heap of feathers, in one close room, with four people absorbing what air there was. "I am afraid,"

I said, "that if it does not soon get some fresh air it will not live. I wonder what would happen to my children if I kept them in one hot room day and night for six months. You see how they are out all day, and how well they are."

"They are so strong," she said with a doleful sniff, "that they can stand it."

I was confounded by this way of looking at it, and turned away, after once more begging her to take the child out. She plainly regarded the advice as brutal, and I heard her blowing her nose all down the drive. In June the father told me he would like the doctor ; the child grew thinner every day in spite of all the food it took. A doctor was got from the nearest town, and I went across to hear what he ordered. He ordered bottles at regular intervals instead of the unbroken series it had been having, and fresh air. He could find nothing the matter with it, except unusual weakness. He asked if it always perspired as it was doing then, and himself took off the topmost bag of feathers. Early in July it died, and its first outing was to the cemetery in the pine woods three miles off.

"I took such care of it," moaned the mother, when I went to try and comfort her after the

funeral; "it would never have lived so long but
for the care I took of it."

"And what the doctor ordered did no good?"
I ventured to ask, as gently as I could.

"Oh, I did not take it out—how could I—
it would have killed it at once—at least I have
kept it alive till now." And she flung her arms
across the table, and burying her head in them
wept bitterly.

There is a great wall of ignorance and prejudice
dividing us from the people on our place, and in
every effort to help them we knock against it and
cannot move it any more than if it were actual
stone. Like the parson on the subject of morals,
I can talk till I am hoarse on the subject of health,
without at any time producing the faintest impression. When things are very bad the doctor is
brought, directions are given, medicines made up,
and his orders, unless they happen to be approved
of, are simply not carried out. Orders to wash
a patient and open windows are never obeyed,
because the whole village would rise up if, later
on, the illness ended in death, and accuse the
relatives of murder. I suppose they regard us
and our like who live on the other side of the
dividing wall as persons of fantastic notions which,

when carried into effect among our own children, do no harm because of the vast strength of the children accumulated during years of eating in the quantities only possible to the rich. Their idea of happiness is eating, and they naturally suppose that everybody eats as much as he can possibly afford to buy. Some of them have known hunger, and food and strength are coupled together in their experience—the more food the greater the strength ; and people who eat roast meat (oh, bliss ineffable !) every day of their lives can bear an amount of washing and airing that would surely kill such as themselves. But how useless to try and discover what their views really are. I can imagine what I like about them, and am fairly certain to imagine wrong. I have no real conception of their attitude towards life, and all I can do is to talk to them kindly when they are in trouble, and as often as I can give them nice things to eat. Shocked at the horrors that must surround the poor women at the birth of their babies, I asked the Man of Wrath to try and make some arrangement that would ensure their quiet at those times. He put aside a little cottage at the end of the street as a home for them in their confinements, and I furnished it, and made it clean and bright and pretty. A nurse was permanently engaged, and I thought with delight of the unspeakable blessing and comfort it was going to be. Not a baby has been born in that cottage, for not a woman has allowed herself to be taken there. At the end of a year it had to be let out again to families, and the nurse dismissed.

"*Why* wouldn't they go?" I asked the Frau Inspector, completely puzzled. She shrugged her shoulders. "They like their husband and children round them," she said, "and are afraid something will be done to them away from home—that they will be washed too often, perhaps. The gracious lady will never get them to leave their homes." "The gracious lady gives it up," I muttered.

When I opened the next door I was bewildered by the crowd in the room. A woman stood in the middle at a wash-tub which took up most of the space. Every now and then she put out a dripping hand and jerked a perambulator up and down for a moment, to calm the shrieks of the baby inside. On a wooden bench at the foot of one of the three beds a very old man sat and blinked at nothing. Crouching in a corner were two small boys of pasty complexion, playing with a guinea-pig and coughing violently. The loveliest

little girl I have seen for a very long while lay in
the bed nearest the door, quite silent, with her
eyes closed and her mouth shut tight, as though
she were trying hard to bear something. As I
pulled the door open the first thing I saw, right
up against it, was this set young face framed in
tossed chestnut hair. "Why, *Frauchen*," I said
to the woman at the tub, "so many of you at
home to-day? Are you all ill?" There was
hardly standing room for an extra person, and the
room was full of steam.

"They have all got the cough I had," she
answered, without looking up, "and Lotte there is
very bad."

I took Lotte's rough little hand—so different
from the delicate face—and found she was in a fever.

"We must get the doctor," I said.

"Oh, the doctor—" said the mother with a
shrug, "he's no use."

"You must do what he tells you, or he cannot
help you."

"That last medicine he sent me all but killed
me," she said, washing vigorously. "I'll never
take any more of his, nor shall any child of mine."

"What medicine was it?"

She wiped her hand on her apron, and reaching

across to the cupboard took out a little bottle. "I was in bed two days after it," she said, handing it to me—"as though I were dead, not knowing what was going on round me." The bottle had contained opium, and there were explicit directions written on it as to the number of drops to be taken and the length of the intervals between the taking.

"Did you do exactly what is written here?" I asked.

"I took it all at once. There wasn't much of it, and I was feeling bad."

"But then of course it nearly killed you. I wonder it didn't quite. What good is it our taking all the trouble we do to send that long distance for the doctor if you don't do as he orders?"

"I'll take no more of his medicine. If it had been any good and able to cure me, the more I took the quicker I ought to have been cured." And she scrubbed and thumped with astounding energy, while Lotte lay with her little ashen face a shade more set and suffering. The wash-tub, though in the middle of the room, was quite close to Lotte's bed, because the middle of the room was quite close to every other part of it, and each extra hard maternal thump must have hit the child's head like a blow from a hammer. She was, you see, only thirteen, and her skin had not had time to turn into leather.

"Has this child eaten anything to-day?"

"She won't."

"Is she not thirsty?"

"She won't drink coffee or milk."

"I'll send her something she may like, and I shall send, too, for the doctor."

"I'll not give her his stuff."

"Let me beg you to do as he tells you."

"I'll not give her his stuff."

"Was it absolutely necessary to wash to-day?"

"It's the day."

"My good woman," said I to myself, gazing at her with outward blandness, "I'd like exceedingly to tip you up into your wash-tub and thump you as thoroughly as you are thumping those unfortunate clothes." Aloud I said in flute-like tones of conciliation, "Good afternoon."

"Good afternoon," said she without looking up.

Washing days always mean tempers, and I ought to have fled at the first sight of that tub, but then there was Lotte in her little yellow flannel night-gown, suffering as only children can suffer, helpless, forced to patience, forced to silent endurance of any banging and vehemence in which her

mother might choose to indulge. No wonder her
mouth was shut like a clasp and she would not
open her eyes. Her eyebrows were reddish like
her hair, and very straight, and her eyelashes lay
dusky and long on her white face. At least I had
discovered Lotte and could help her a little, I
thought, as I departed down the garden path
between the rows of scarlet runners; but the help
that takes the form of jelly and iced drinks is not
of a lasting nature, and I have but little sympathy
with a benevolence that finds its highest expression
in gifts of the kind. There have been women
within my experience who went down into the
grave accompanied by special pastoral encomiums,
and whose claims to lady-bountifulness, on closer
inquiry, rested solely on a foundation of jelly.
Yet nothing in the world is easier than ordering
jelly to be sent to the sick, except refraining from
ordering it. What more, however, could I do for
Lotte than this? I could not take her up in my
arms and run away with her and nurse her back to
health, for she would probably object to such a
course as strongly as her mother; and later on,
when she gets well again, she will go back to school,
and grow coarse and bouncing and leathery like the
others, affording the parson, in three or four years'

time, a fresh occasion for grief over deadly sin. "If one could only get hold of the children!" I sighed, as I went up the steps into the school-house; "catch them young, and put them in a garden, with no older people of their own class for ever teaching them by example what is ugly, and unworthy, and gross."

Afternoon school was going on, and the assistant teacher was making the children read aloud in turns In winter, when they would be glad of a warm, roomy place in which to spend their afternoons, school is only in the morning; and in summer, when the thirstiest after knowledge are apt to be less keen, it is both morning and afternoon. The arrangement is so mysterious that it must be providential. Herr Schenk, the head master, was away giving my babies their daily lessons, and his assistant, a youth in spectacles but yet of pugnacious aspect, was sitting in the master's desk, exercising a pretty turn for sarcasm in his running comments on the reading. A more complete waste of breath and brilliancy can hardly be imagined. He is not yet, however, married, and marriage is a great chastener. The children all stood up when I came in, and the teacher ceased sharpening his wits on a dulness that could not feel, and with many bows put a chair for me and begged me to sit on it. I did sit on it, and asked that they might go on with the lesson, as I had only come in for a minute on my way down the street. The reading was accordingly resumed, but unaccompanied this time by sarcasms. What faces! What dull, apathetic, low, coarse faces! On one side sat those from ten to fourteen, with not a hopeful face among them, and on the other those from six to ten, with one single little boy who looked as though he could have no business among the rest, so bright was he, so attentive, so curiously dignified. Poor children —what could the parson hope to make of beings whose expressions told so plainly of the sort of nature within? Those that did not look dull looked cunning, and all the girls on the older side had the faces of women. I began to feel dreadfully depressed. "See what you have done," I whispered angrily to my conscience—"made me wretched without doing anybody else any good." "The old woman with the headache is happy in the hopes of grapes," it replied, seeking to justify itself, "and Lotte is to have some jelly." "Grapes! Jelly! Futility unutterable. I can't bear this, and am going home." The teacher inquired whether the children should sing something to my graciousness:

perhaps he was ashamed of their reading, and indeed I never heard anything like it. "Oh yes," I said, resigned, but outwardly smiling kindly with the self-control natural to woman. They sang, or rather screamed, a hymn, and so frightfully loud and piercingly that the very windows shook. "My dear," explained the Man of Wrath, when I complained one Sunday on our way home from church of the terrible quality and volume of the music, "it frightens scoffers away."

Our numerous godchildren were not in school because, as we have only lived here three years, they are not yet old enough to share in the blessings of education. I stand godparent to the girls, and the Man of Wrath to the boys, and as all the babies are accordingly named after us the village swarms with tiny Elizabeths and Boys of Wrath. A hunchbacked woman, unfit for harder work, looks after the babies during the day in a room set apart for that purpose, so that the mothers may not be hampered in their duties at the farm ; they have only to carry the babies there in the morning, and fetch them away again in the evening, and can feel that they are safe and well looked after. But many of them, for some reason too cryptic to fathom, prefer to lock them up in their room, exposed to all the perils that surround an inquiring child just able to walk, and last winter one little creature was burnt to death, sacrificed to her mother's stupidity. This mother, a fair type of the intelligence prevailing in the village, made a great fire in her room before going out, so that when she came back at noon there would still be some with which to cook the dinner, left a baby in a perambulator, and a little Elizabeth of three loose in the room, locked the door, put the key in her pocket, and went off to work. When she came back to get the dinner ready the baby was still crowing placidly in its perambulator, and the little Elizabeth, with all the clothes burnt off her body, was lying near the grate dead. Of course the mother was wild with grief, distracted, raving, desperate, and of course all the other women were shocked and horrified ; but point the moral as we might, we could not bring them to see that it was an avoidable misfortune with nothing whatever to do with the *Finger Gottes*, and the mothers who preferred locking their babies up alone to sending them to be looked after, went on doing so as undisturbed as though what had oc- curred could in no wise be a lesson to themselves.

"Pray, *Herr Lehrer*, why are those two little

boys sitting over there on that seat all by themselves and not singing?" I asked at the conclusion of the hymn.

"That, gracious lady, is the vermin bench. It is necessary to keep——"

"Oh yes, yes—I quite understand—good afternoon. Good-bye, children, you have sung very nicely indeed."

"Now," said I to myself, when I was safely out in the street again, "I am going home."

"Oh, not yet," at once protested my unmanageable conscience; "your favourite old woman lives in the next cottage, and surely you are not going to leave her out?"

"I see plainly," I replied, "that I shall never be quite comfortable till I have got rid of *you*," and in I went to the next house.

The entrance was full of three women—the entrances here are narrow, and the women wide—and they all looked more cheerful than seemed reasonable. They stood aside to let me pass, and when I opened the door I found the room equally full of women, looking equally happy, and talking eagerly.

"Why, what is happening?" I asked the nearest one. "Is there a party?"

She turned round, grinning broadly in obvious delight. "The old lady died in her sleep," she said, "and was found this morning dead in her bed. I was in here only yesterday, and she said——" I turned abruptly and went out again. All those gloating women, hovering round the poor body that was clothed on a sudden by death with a wonderful dignity and nobleness, made me ashamed of being a woman. Not a man was there,—clearly a superior race of beings. In the entrance I met the Frau Inspector coming in to arrange matters, and she turned and walked with me a little way.

"The old lady was better off than we thought," she remarked, "and has left a very good black silk dress to be buried in."

"A black silk dress?" I repeated.

"And everything to match in goodness—nice leather shoes, good stockings, under-things all trimmed with crochet, real whalebone corsets, and a quite new pair of white kid gloves. She must have saved for a long time to have it all so nice."

"But," I said, "I don't understand. I have never had anything to do yet with death, and have not thought of these things. Are not people, then, just buried in a shroud?"

" A shroud? " It was her turn not to under-stand.

" A sheet sort of thing."

She smiled in a highly superior manner. " Oh dear, no," she said, " we are none of us quite so poor as that."

I glanced down at her as she walked beside me. She is a short woman, and carries weight. She was smiling almost pityingly at my ignorance of what is due, even after death, to ourselves and public opinion.

" The very poorest," she said, " manage to scrape a whole set of clothes together for their funerals. A very poor couple came here a few months ago, and before the man had time to earn anything he died. The wife came to me (the gracious lady was absent), and on her knees implored me to give her a suit for him—she had only been able to afford the *Sterbehemd*, and was frantic at the thought of what the neighbours would say if he had nothing on but that, and said she would be haunted by shame and remorse all the rest of her life. We bought a nice black suit, and tie, and gloves, and he really looked very well. She will be dressed to-night," she went on, as I said nothing ; " the dressers come with the coffin, and it will be a nice funeral. I used to wonder what she did with her pension money, and never could persuade her to buy herself a bit of meat. But of course she was saving for this. They are beautiful corsets."

"What utter waste!" I ejaculated.

"Waste?"

"Yes—utter waste and foolishness. Foolishness, not to have bought a few little comforts, waste of the money, and waste of the clothes. Is there any meaning, sense, or use whatever in burying a good black silk dress?"

"It would be a scandal not to be buried decently," she replied, manifestly surprised at my warmth, "and the neighbours respect her much more now that they know what nice clothes she had bought for her funeral. Nothing is wanting. I even found a box with a gold brooch in it, and a bracelet."

"I suppose, then, as many of her belongings as will go into the coffin will be buried too, in order to still further impress the neighbours?" I asked—"her feather bed, for instance, and anything else of use and value?"

"No, only what she has on, and the brushes and combs and towels that were used in dressing her."

"How ugly and how useless!" I said with a shiver of disgust.

"It is the custom," was her tranquil reply.

Suddenly an unpleasant thought struck me, and I burst out emphatically, "Nothing but a shroud is to be put on me."

"Oh no," she said, looking up at me with a face meant to be full of the most reassuring promises of devotion, "the gracious lady may be quite certain that if I am still here she will have on her most beautiful ball dress and finest linen, and that the whole neighbourhood shall see for themselves how well *Herrschaften* know what is due to them."

"I shall give directions," I repeated with increased energy, "that there is only to be a shroud."

"Oh no, no," she protested, smiling as though she were humouring a spoilt and eccentric child, "such a thing could never be permitted. What would our feelings be when we remembered that the gracious lady had not received her dues, and what would the neighbours say?"

"I'll have nothing but a shroud!" I cried in great wrath—and then stopped short, and burst out laughing. "What an absurd and gruesome conversation," I said, holding out my hand.

"Good-bye, Frau Inspector, I am sure you are wanted in that cottage."

She made me a curtsey and turned back. I walked out of the village and through the fir wood and the meadow as quickly as I could, opened the gate into my garden, went down the most sheltered path, flung myself on the grass in a quiet nook, and said aloud "Ugh!"

It is a well-known exclamation of disgust, and is thus inadequately expressed in writing.

August

AUGUST

August 5th.—August has come, and has clothed the hills with golden lupins, and filled the grassy banks with harebells. The yellow fields of lupins are so gorgeous on cloudless days that I have neglected the forests lately and drive in the open, so that I may revel in their scent while feasting my eyes on their beauty. The slope of a hill clothed with this orange wonder and seen against the sky is one of those sights which make me so happy that it verges on pain. The straight, vigorous flower-spikes are something like hyacinths, but all aglow with a divine intensity of brightness that a yellow hyacinth never yet possessed and never will; and then they are not waxy, but velvety, and their leaves are not futile drooping things, but delicate, strong sprays of an exquisite grey-green, with a bloom on them that throws a mist over the whole field ; and as for the perfume, it surely is the perfume of Paradise. The plant is altogether lovely—shape, growth, flower, and leaf, and the horses have to wait very patiently once we get among them, for I can never have enough of sitting quite still in those fair fields of glory. Not far from here there is a low series of hills running north and south, absolutely without trees, and at the foot of them, on the east side, is a sort of road, chiefly stones, but yet with patience to be driven over, and on the other side of this road a plain stretches away towards the east and south ; and hills and plain are now one sheet of gold. I have driven there at all hours of the day —I cannot keep away—and I have seen them early in the morning, and at mid-day, and in the afternoon, and I have seen them in the evening by moonlight, when all the intensity was washed out of the colour and into the scent; but just as the sun drops behind the little hills is the supreme moment, when the splendour is so dazzling that you feel as though you must have reached the very gates of heaven. So strong was this feeling the other day that I actually got out of the carriage, being impulsive, and began almost in-

voluntarily to climb the hill, half expecting to see
the glories of the New Jerusalem all spread out
before me when I should reach the top ; and it
came with quite a shock of disappointment to find
there was nothing there but the prose of potato-
fields, and a sandy road with home-going calves
kicking up its dust, and in the distance our
neighbour's *Schloss*, and the New Jerusalem just
as far off as ever.

It is a relief to me to write about these things
that I so much love, for I do not talk of them lest
I should be regarded as a person who rhapsodizes,
and there is no nuisance more intolerable than
having somebody's rhapsodies thrust upon you
when you have no enthusiasm of your own that at
all corresponds. I know this so well that I generally succeed in keeping quiet ; but sometimes even
now, after years of study in the art of holding my
tongue, some stray fragment of what I feel does
occasionally come out, and then I am at once pulled
up and brought to my senses by the well-known
cold stare of utter incomprehension, or the look of
indulgent superiority that awaits any exposure of
a feeling not in the least understood. How is it
that you should feel so vastly superior whenever
you do not happen to enter into or understand

your neighbour's thoughts when, as a matter of
fact, your not being able to do so is less a sign of
folly in your neighbour than of incompleteness in
yourself? I am quite sure that if I were to take
most or any of my friends to those pleasant yellow
fields they would notice nothing except the exceeding joltiness of the road ; and if I were so ill-
advised as to lift up a corner of my heart, and let
them see how full it was of wonder and delight,
they would first look blank, and then decide
mentally that they were in the unpleasant situation
of driving over a stony road with that worst form
of idiot, a bore, and so fall into the mood of self-
commiseration which is such a solace to us in our
troubles. Yet it is painful being suppressed for
ever and ever, and I believe the torments of such
a state, when unduly prolonged, are more keenly
felt by a woman than a man, she having, in spite
of her protestations, a good deal of the ivy nature
still left in her, and an unhealthy craving for
sympathy and support. When I drive to the
lupins and see them all spread out as far as eye
can reach in perfect beauty of colour and scent
and bathed in the mild August sunshine, I feel I
must send for somebody to come and look at them
with me, and talk about them to me, and share in

the pleasure ; and when I run over the list of my
friends and try to find one who would enjoy them,
I am frightened once more at the solitariness in
which we each of us live. I have, it is true, a
great many friends—people with whom it is pleasant
to spend an afternoon if such afternoons are not
repeated often, and if you are careful not to stir
more than the surface of things, but among them
all there is only one who has, roughly, the same
tastes that I have ; and even her sympathies have
limitations, and she declares for instance with
emphasis that she would not at all like to be a
goose-girl. I wonder why. Our friendship nearly
came to an end over the goose-girl, so unexpectedly
inflaming did the subject turn out to be. Of all
professions, if I had liberty of choice, I would
choose to be a gardener, and if nobody would have
me in that capacity I would like to be a goose-girl,
and sit in the greenest of fields minding those
delightfully plump, placid geese, whiter and more
leisurely than the clouds on a calm summer morning,
their very waddle in its lazy deliberation soothing
and salutary to a fretted spirit that has been too
long on the stretch. The fields geese feed in are
so specially charming, so green and low-lying, with
little clumps of trees and bushes, and a pond or

boggy bit of ground somewhere near, and a pro-
fusion of those delicate field flowers that look so
lovely growing and are so unsatisfactory and fade
so quickly if you try to arrange them in your
rooms. For six months of the year I would be
happier than any queen I ever heard of, minding
the fat white things.   I would begin in April with
the king-cups, and leave off in September with the
blackberries, and I would keep one eye on the
geese, and one on the volume of Wordsworth I
should have with me, and I would be present in
this way at the procession of the months, the first
three all white and yellow, and the last three
gorgeous with the lupin fields and the blues and
purples and crimsons that clothe the hedges and
ditches in a wonderful variety of shades, and dye
the grass near the water in great patches.   Then
in October I would shut up my Wordsworth, go
back to civilised life, and probably assist at the
eating of the geese one after the other, with a
proper thankfulness for the amount of edification
I had from first to last extracted from them.

I believe in England goose eating is held to be
of doubtful refinement, and is left to one's servants.
Here roast goose stuffed with apples is a dish
loved quite openly and simply by people who

would consider that the number of their quarterings
raises them above any suspicion as to the refinement of their tastes, however many geese they
may eat, and however much they may enjoy them ;
and I remember one lady, whose ancestors, probably
all having loved goose, reached back up to a quite
giddy antiquity, casting a gloom over a dinner-
table by removing as much of the skin or crackling
of the goose as she could when it came to her,
remarking, amidst a mournful silence, that it was
her favourite part. No doubt it was. The
misfortune was that it happened also to be the
favourite part of the line of guests who came after
her, and who saw themselves forced by the hard
laws of propriety to affect an indifferent dignity of
bearing at the very moment when their one feeling
was a fierce desire to rise up and defend at all
costs their right to a share of skin. She had, I
remember, very pretty little white hands like tiny
claws, and wore beautiful rings, and sitting opposite
her, and free myself from any undue passion for
goose, I had leisure to watch the rapid way in
which she disposed of the skin, her rings and the
whiteness of her hands flashing up and down as
she used her knife and fork with the awful dexterity
only seen in perfection in the Fatherland. I am

afraid that as a nation we think rather more of our eating and drinking than is reasonable, and this no doubt explains why so many of us, by the time we are thirty, have lost the original classicality of our contour. Walking in the streets of a town you are almost sure to catch the word *essen* in the talk of the passers-by ; and *das Essen*, combined, of course, with the drinking made necessary by its exaggerated indulgence, constitutes the chief happiness of the middle and lower classes. Any story-book or novel you take up is full of feeling descriptions of what everybody ate and drank, and there are a great many more meals than kisses ; so that the novel-reader who expects a love-tale, finds with disgust that he is put off with *menus*. The upper classes have so many other amusements that *das Essen* ceases to be one, and they are as thin as all the rest of the world ; but if the curious wish to see how very largely it fills the lives, or that part of their lives that they reserve for pleasure, of the middle classes, it is a good plan to go to seaside places during the months of July and August, when the schools close, and the *bourgeoisie* realises the dream in which it has been indulging the whole year, of hotel life with a tremendous dinner every day at one o'clock.

The April baby was a weak little creature
in her first years, and the doctor ordered as
specially bracing a seaside resort frequented
solely by the middle classes, and there for three
succeeding years I took her ; and while she rolled
on the sands and grew brown and lusty, I was
dull, and fell to watching the other tourists.
Their time, it appeared, was spent in ruminating
over the delights of the meal that was eaten, and
in preparing their bodies by gentlest exercise for
the delights of the meal that was to come. They
passed their mornings on the sands, the women
doing fancy work in order that they might look
busy, and the men strolling aimlessly about near
them with field-glasses, and nautical caps, and
long cloaks of a very dreadful pattern reaching to
their heels and making them look like large
women, called Havelocks,—all of them waiting
with more or less open eagerness for one o'clock,
the great moment to which they had been looking
forward ever since the day before, to arrive.
They used to file in when the bell rang with a
sort of silent solemnity, a contemplative collected-
ness, which is best described by the word *recueille-
ment*, and ate all the courses, however many there
were, in a hot room full of flies and sunlight.

The dinner lasted a good hour and a half, and at the end of that time they would begin to straggle out again, flushed and using toothpicks as they strolled to the tables under the trees, where the exhausted waiters would presently bring them breakfast-cups of coffee and cakes. They lingered about an hour over this, and then gradually disappeared to their rooms, where they slept, I suppose, for from then till about six a death-like stillness reigned in the place, and April and I had it all to ourselves. Towards six, slow couples would be seen crawling along the path by the shore and panting up into the woods, this being the only exercise of the day, and necessary if they would eat their suppers with appreciation; and April and I, peering through the bracken out of the nests of moss we used to make in the afternoons, could see them coming up through the trees after the climb up the cliff, the husband with his Havelock over his arm, a little in front, wiping his face and gasping, the wife in her tight silk dress, her bonnet strings undone, a cloak and an umbrella, and very often a small mysterious basket as well to carry, besides holding up her dress, very stout and very uncomfortable and very breathless, panting along behind; and however

much she had to carry, and however fat and
helpless she was, and however steep the hill, and
however much dinner she had eaten, the idea that
her husband might have taken her cloak and her
umbrella and her basket and carried them for her
would never have struck either of them. If it
had by some strange chance entered his head, he
would have reasoned that he was as stout as she
was, that he had eaten as much dinner, that he
was several years older, and that it was her cloak.
Logic is so irresistible.

To go on eating long after you have ceased to
be hungry has fascinations, apparently, that are
difficult to withstand, and if it gives you so much
pleasure that the resulting inability to move without
gasping is accepted with the meekness of martyrs,
who shall say that you are wrong? My not
myself liking a large dinner at one o'clock is not
a reason for my thinking I am superior to those
who do. Their excesses, it is true, are not my
excesses, but then neither are mine theirs; and
what about the days of idleness I spend, doing
nothing from early till late but lie on the grass
watching clouds? If I were to murmur gluttons,
could not they, from their point of view, retort
with conviction fool? All those maxims about

judging others by yourself, and putting yourself
in another person's place, are not, I am afraid,
reliable. I had them dinned into me constantly
as a child, and I was constantly trying to obey
them, and constantly was astonished at the unexpected results I arrived at ; and now I know
that it is a proof of artlessness to suppose that
other people will think and feel and hope and
enjoy what you do and in the same way that you
do.   If an officious friend had stood in that
breathless couple's path and told them in glowing
terms how much happier they would be if they
lived their life a little more fully and from its
other sides, how much more delightful to stride
along gaily together in their walks, with wind
enough for talk and laughter, how pleasant if the
man were muscular and in good condition and
the woman brisk and wiry, and that they only had
to do as he did and live on cold meat and toast,
and drink nothing, to be as blithe as birds, do
you think they would have so much as understood
him?   Cold meat and toast?   Instead of what
they had just been enjoying so intensely?   Miss
that soup made of the inner mysteries of geese,
those eels stewed in beer, the roast pig with red
cabbage, the venison basted with sour cream and

served with beans in vinegar and cranberry jam,
the piled-up masses of vanilla ice, the pumpernickel
and cheese, the apples and pears on the top of
that, and the big cups of coffee and cakes on the
top of the apples and pears? Really a quick walk
over the heather with a wiry wife would hardly
make up for the loss of such a dinner; and
besides, might not a wiry wife turn out to be a
questionable blessing? And so they would pity
the nimble friend who wasted his life in taking
exercise and missed all its pleasures, and the man
of toast and early rising would regard them with
profound disgust if simple enough to think himself
better than they, and, if he possessed an open
mind, would merely return their pity with more
of his own; so that, I suppose, everybody would
be pleased, for the charm of pitying one's neighbour, though subtle, is undeniable.

I remember when I was at the age when people
began to call me *Backfisch*, and my mother dressed
me in a little scarlet coat with big pearl buttons,
and my eyes turned down because I was shy, and
my nose turned up because I was impudent, one
summer at the seaside with my governess we
noticed in our walks a solitary lady of dignified
appearance, who spoke to no one, and seemed

for ever wrapped in distant and lofty philosophic speculations. "She's thinking about Kant and the nebular hypothesis," I decided to myself, having once heard some men with long beards talking of both those things, and they all had had that same far-away look in their eyes. "*Qu'est-ce que c'est une hypothèse nébuleuse, Mademoiselle?*" I said aloud.

"*Tenez-vous bien, et marchez d'une façon convenable,*" she replied sharply.

"*Qu'est-ce que c'est une hypothèse——*"

"*Vous êtes trop jeune pour comprendre ces choses.*"

"*Oh alors vous ne savez pas vous-même!*" I cried triumphantly, "*Sans cela vous me diriez.*"

"*Élisabeth, vous écrirez, dès que nous rentrons, le verbe Prier le bon Dieu de m'Aider à ne plus Être si Impertinente.*"

She was an ingenious young woman, and the verbs I had to write as punishments were of the most elaborate and complicated nature—*Demander pardon pour Avoir Sifflé comme un Gamin quelconque, Vouloir ne plus Oublier de Nettoyer mes Ongles, Essayer de ne pas tant Aimer les Poudings,* are but a few examples of her achievements in this particular branch of discipline.

That very day at the *table d'hôte* the abstracted lady sat next to me. A *ragoût* of some sort was handed round, and after I had taken some she asked me, before helping herself, what it was.

"Snails," I replied promptly, wholly unchastened by the prayers I had just been writing out in every tense.

"Snails! *Ekelig*." And she waved the waiter loftily away, and looked on with much superciliousness at the rest of us enjoying ourselves.

"What! You do not eat this excellent *ragoût?*' asked her other neighbour, a hot man, as he finished clearing his plate and had time to observe the emptiness of hers. "You do not like calves' tongues and mushrooms? *Sonderbar*."

I still can see the poor lady's face as she turned on me more like a tigress than the impassive person she had been a moment before. "*Sie unverschämter Backfisch!*" she hissed. "My favourite dish—I have you to thank for spoiling my repast—my day!" And in a frenzy of rage she gripped my arm as though she would have shaken me then and there in the face of the multitude, while I sat appalled at the consequences of indulging a playful fancy at the wrong time.

Which story, now I come to think of it, illustrates less the tremendous importance of food in our country than the exceeding odiousness of *Backfische* in scarlet coats.

August 16th.—My idea of a garden is that it should be beautiful from end to end, and not start off in front of the house with fireworks, going off at its farthest limit into sheer sticks. The standard reached beneath the windows should at least be kept up, if it cannot be surpassed, right away through, and the German popular plan in this matter quite discarded of concentrating all the available splendour of the establishment into the supreme effort of carpet-bedding and glass balls on pedestals in front of the house, in the hope that the stranger, carefully kept in that part, and on no account allowed to wander, will infer an equal magnificence throughout the entire domain; whereas he knows very well all the time that the landscape round the corner consists of fowls and dust-bins. Disliking this method, I have tried to make my garden increase in loveliness, if not in tidiness, the farther you get into it; and the visitor who thinks in his innocence as he emerges from the shade of the verandah that he sees the best before him, is artfully conducted from beauty to beauty till he beholds what I think is the most charming bit, the silver birch and azalea plantation down at the very end. This is the boundary of my kingdom on the south side, a blaze of colour in May and June, across which you see the placid meadows stretching away to a distant wood ; and from its contemplation the ideal visitor returns to the house a refreshed and better man. That is the sort of person one enjoys taking round—the man (or woman) who, loving gardens, would go any distance to see one ; who comes to appreciate, and compare, and admire ; who has a garden of his own that he lives in and loves ; and whose talk and criticisms are as dew to the thirsty gardening soul, all too accustomed in this respect to droughts. He knows as well as I do what work, what patience, what study and watching, what laughter at failures, what fresh starts with undiminished zeal, and what bright, unalterable faith are represented by the flowers in my garden. He knows what I have done for it, and he knows what it has done for me, and how it has been and will be more and more a place of joys, a place of lessons, a place of health, a place of miracles, and a place of sure and never-changing peace.

Living face to face with nature makes it difficult for one to be discouraged. Moles and late frosts, both of which are here in abundance, have often grieved and disappointed me, but even these, my worst enemies, have not succeeded in making me feel discouraged. Not once till now have I got farther in that direction than the purely negative state of not being encouraged ; and whenever I reach that state I go for a brisk walk in the sunshine and come back cured. It makes one so healthy to live in a garden, so healthy in mind as well as body, and when I say moles and late frosts are my worst enemies, it only shows how I could not now if I tried sit down and brood over my own or my neighbour's sins, and how the breezes in my garden have blown away all those worries and vexations and bitternesses that are the lot of those who live in a crowd. The most severe frost that ever nipped the hopes of a year is better to my thinking than having to listen to one malignant truth or lie, and I would rather have a mole busy burrowing tunnels under each of my rose trees and letting the air get at their roots than face a single greeting where no kindness is. How can you help being happy if you are healthy and in the place you want to be ? A man once made it a reproach that

I should be so happy, and told me everybody has crosses, and that we live in a vale of woe. I mentioned moles as my principal cross, and pointed to the huge black mounds with which they had decorated the tennis-court, but I could not agree to the vale of woe, and could not be shaken in my belief that the world is a dear and lovely place, with everything in it to make us happy so long as we walk humbly and diet ourselves. He pointed out that sorrow and sickness were sure to come, and seemed quite angry with me when I suggested that they too could be borne perhaps with cheerfulness. "And have not even such things their sunny side?" I exclaimed. "When I am steeped to the lips in diseases and doctors, I shall at least have something to talk about that interests my women friends, and need not sit as I do now wondering what I shall say next and wishing they would go." He replied that all around me lay misery, sin, and suffering, and that every person not absolutely blinded by selfishness must be aware of it and must realise the seriousness and tragedy of existence. I asked him whether my being miserable and discontented would help any one or make him less wretched; and he said that we all had to take up our burdens. I assured him I would not shrink from mine, though I felt secretly ashamed of it when I remembered that it was only moles, and he went away with a grave face and a shaking head, back to his wife and his eleven children. I heard soon afterwards that a twelfth baby had been born and his wife had died, and in dying had turned her face with a quite unaccountable impatience away from him and to the wall; and the rumour of his piety reached even into my garden, and how he had said, as he closed her eyes, "It is the Will of God." He was a missionary.

But of what use is it telling a woman with a garden that she ought really to be ashamed of herself for being happy? The fresh air is so buoyant that it lifts all remarks of that sort away off you and leaves you laughing. They get wafted away on the scent of the stocks, and you stand in the sun looking round at your cheerful flowers, and more than ever persuaded that it is a good and blessed thing to be thankful. Oh a garden is a sweet, sane refuge to have! Whether I am tired because I have enjoyed myself too much, or tired because I have lectured the servants too much, or tired because I have talked to missionaries too much, I have only to come down the verandah steps into the garden to be at once restored to

quiet, and serenity, and my real and natural self.
I could almost fancy sometimes that as I come
down the steps, gentle hands of blessing have
been laid on my head. I suppose I feel so because
of the hush that descends on my soul when I get
out of the close, restless house into that silent purity.

Sometimes I sit for hours in the south walk
by the verandah just listening and watching. It
is so private there, though directly beneath the
windows, that it is one of my favourite places.
There are no bedrooms on that side of the house,
only the Man of Wrath's and my day-rooms, so
that servants cannot see me as I stand there
enjoying myself. If they did or could, I should
simply never go there, for nothing is so utterly
destructive to meditation as to know that probably
somebody inquisitive is eyeing you from behind a
curtain. The loveliest garden I know is spoilt to
my thinking by the impossibility of getting out
of sight of the house, which stares down at you,
Argus-eyed and unblinking, into whatever corner
you may shuffle. Perfect house and perfect garden,
lying in that land of lovely gardens, England, the
garden just the right size for perfection, not a
weed ever admitted, every dandelion and daisy—
those friends of the unaspiring—routed out years

ago, the borders exquisite examples of taste, the turf so faultless that you hardly like to walk on it for fear of making it dusty, and the whole quite uninhabitable for people of my solitary tendencies because, go where you will, you are overlooked. Since I have lived in this big straggling place, full of paths and copses where I am sure of being left alone, with wide fields and heath and forests beyond, and so much room to move and breathe in, I feel choked, oppressed, suffocated, in anything small and perfect. I spent a very happy afternoon in that little English paradise, but I came away quite joyfully, and with many a loving thought of my own dear ragged garden, and all the corners in it where the anemones twinkle in the spring like stars, and where there is so much nature and so little art. It will grow I know sweeter every year, but it is too big ever to be perfect and to get to look so immaculate that the diseased imagination conjures up visions of housemaids issuing forth each morning in troops and dusting every separate flower with feather brushes. Nature herself is untidy, and in a garden she ought to come first, and Art with her brooms and clipping-shears follow humbly behind. Art has such a good time in the house, where she spreads herself over the

walls, and hangs herself up gorgeously at the
windows, and lurks in the sofa cushions, and
breaks out in an eruption of pots wherever pots
are possible, that really she should be content to
take the second place out of doors. And how
dreadful to meet a gardener and a wheelbarrow at
every turn—which is precisely what happens to
one in the perfect garden. My gardener, whose
deafness is more than compensated for by the
keenness of his eyesight, very soon remarked the
scowl that distorted my features whenever I met
one of his assistants in my favourite walks, and I
never meet them now. I think he must keep
them chained up to the cucumber-frames, so
completely have they disappeared, and he only
lets them loose when he knows I am driving, or
at meals, or in bed. But is it not irritating to be
sitting under your favourite tree, pencil in hand,
and eyes turned skywards expectant of the spark
from heaven that never falls, and then to have a
man appear suddenly round the corner who immediately begins quite close to you to tear up the
earth with his fangs? No one will ever know
the number of what I believe are technically
known as winged words that I have missed
bringing down through interruptions of this kind.

Indeed, as I look through these pages I see I must have missed them all, for I can find nothing anywhere with even a rudimentary approach to wings.

Sometimes when I am in a critical mood and need all my faith to keep me patient, I shake my head at the unshornness of the garden as gravely as the missionary shook his head at me. The bushes stretch across the paths, and, catching at me as I go by, remind me that they have not been pruned; the teeming plant life rejoices on the lawns free from all interference from men and hoes; the pinks are closely nibbled off at the beginning of each summer by selfish hares intent on their own gratification; most of the beds bear the marks of nocturnal foxes; and the squirrels spend their days wantonly biting off and flinging down the tender young shoots of the firs. Then there is the boy who drives the donkey and water-cart round the garden, and who has an altogether reprehensible habit of whisking round corners and slicing off bits of the lawn as he whisks. "But you can't alter these things, my good soul," I say to myself. "If you want to get rid of the hares and foxes, you must consent to have wire-netting, which is odious, right round your garden. And you are always saying you like weeds, so why grumble at your lawns? And it doesn't hurt you much if the squirrels do break bits off your firs—the firs must have had that happening to them years and years before you were born, yet they still flourish. As for boys, they certainly are revolting creatures. Can't you catch this one when he isn't looking and pop him in his own water-barrel and put the lid on?"

I asked the June baby, who has several times noticed with indignation the culpable indifference of this boy in regard to corners, whether she did not think that would be a good way of disposing of him. She is a great disciplinarian, and was loud in her praise of the plan; but the other two demurred. "He might go dead in there," said the May baby apprehensively. "And he is such a naughty boy," said April, who had watched his reckless conduct with special disgust, "that if he once went dead he'd go straight to the *Hölle* and stay all the time with the *diable*."

That was the first French word I have heard them say: strange and sulphureous first-fruits of Séraphine's teaching!

We were going round the garden in a procession, I with a big pair of scissors, and the Three with baskets, into one of which I put fresh flowers, and into the others flowers that were beginning to seed, dead flowers, and seed-pods. The garden was quivering in heat and light; rain in the morning had brought out all the snails and all the sweetness, and we were very happy, as we always are, I when I am knee-deep in flowers, and the babies when they can find new sorts of snails to add to their collections. These collections are carried about in cardboard boxes all day, and at night each baby has hers on the chair beside her bed. Sometimes the snails get out and crawl over the beds, but the babies do not mind. Once when April woke in the morning she was overjoyed by finding a friendly little one on her cheek. Clearly babies of iron nerves and pellucid consciences.

"So you do know some French," I said as I snipped off poppy-heads; "you have always pretended you don't."

"Oh, keep the poppies, mummy," cried April, as she saw them tumbling into her basket; "if you picks them and just leaves them, then they ripes and is good for such a many things."

"Tell me about the *diable*," I said, "and you shall keep the poppies."

"He isn't nice, that *diable*," she said, starting

off at once with breathless eloquence. "Séraphine says there was one time a girl and a boy who went for a walk, and there were two ways, and one way goes where stones is, but it goes to the *lieber Gott*; and the girl went that way till she came to a door, and the *lieber Gott* made the door opened and she went in, and that's the *Himmel*."

"And the boy?"

"Oh, he was a naughty boy and went the other way where there is a tree, and on the tree is written, 'Don't go this way or you'll be dead,' and he said, 'That is one *bêtise*,' and did go in the way and got to the *Hölle*, and there he gets whippings when he doesn't make what the *diable* says."

"That's because he was so naughty," explained the May baby, holding up an impressive finger, "and didn't want to go to the *Himmel* and didn't love glory."

"All boys are naughty," said June, "and I don't love them."

"*Nous allons parler Français*," I announced, desirous of finding out whether their whole stock was represented by *diable* and *bêtise*; "I believe you can all speak it quite well."

There was no answer. I snipped off sweet-pea pods and began to talk French at a great rate, asking questions as I snipped, and trying to extract answers, and getting none. The silence behind me grew ominous. Presently I heard a faint sniff, and the basket being held up to me began to shake. I bent down quickly and looked under April's sun-bonnet. She was crying great dreadful tears, and rubbing her eyes hard with her one free hand.

" Why, you most blessed of babies," I exclaimed, kneeling down and putting my arms round her, "what in the world is the matter ? "

She looked at me with grieved and doubting eyes. "Such a mother to talk French to her child !" she sobbed.

I threw down the scissors, picked her up, and carried her up and down the path, comforting her with all the soft words I knew and suppressing my desire to smile. "That's not French, is it ? " I whispered at the end of a long string of endearments, beginning, I believe, with such flights of rhetoric as priceless blessing and angel baby, and ending with a great many kisses.

" No, no," she answered, patting my face and looking infinitely relieved, "that is pretty, and how mummies always talks. Proper mummies never speak French—only Séraphines." And she gave me a very tight hug, and a kiss that transferred all her tears to my face ; and I set her down and, taking out my handkerchief, tried to wipe off the traces of my attempt at governessing from her cheeks. I wonder how it is that whenever babies cry, streaks of mud immediately appear on their faces. I believe I could cry for a week, and yet produce no mud.

"I'll tell you what I'll do, babies," I said, anxious to restore complete serenity on such a lovely day, and feeling slightly ashamed of my uncalled-for zeal—indeed, April was right, and proper mothers leave lessons and torments to somebody else, and devote all their energies to petting —"I'll give a ball after tea."

"*Yes !*" shouted three exultant voices, "and invite all the babies ! "

"So now you must arrange what you are going to wear. I suppose you'd like the same supper as usual ? Run away to Séraphine and tell her to get you ready."

They seized their baskets and their boxes of snails and rushed off into the bushes, calling for Séraphine with nothing but rapture in their voices, and French and the *diable* quite forgotten.

These balls are given with great ceremony two

or three times a year. They last about an hour, during which I sit at the piano in the library playing cheerful tunes, and the babies dance passionately round the pillar. They refuse to waltz together, which is perhaps a good thing, for if they did there would always be one left over to be a wallflower and gnash her teeth ; and when they want to dance squares they are forced by the stubbornness of numbers to dance triangles. At the appointed hour they knock at the door, and come in attired in the garments they have selected as appropriate (at this last ball the April baby wore my shooting coat, the May baby had a muff, and the June baby carried Séraphine's umbrella), and, curtseying to me, each one makes some remark she thinks suitable to the occasion.

"How's your husband ?" June asked me last time, in the defiant tones she seems to think proper at a ball.

"Very well, thank you."

"Oh. That is nice."

"Mine isn't vely well," remarked April cheerfully.

"Indeed ?"

"No, he has got some tummy-aches."

"Dear me !"

"He was coming else, and had such fine twowsers to wear—pink ones with wibbons."

After a little more graceful conversation of this kind the ball begins, and at the end of an hour's dancing, supper, consisting of radishes and lemonade, is served on footstools; and when they have cleared it up even to the leaves and stalks of the radishes, they rise with much dignity, express in proper terms their sense of gratitude for the entertainment, curtsey, and depart to bed, where they spend a night of horror, the prey of the awful dreams naturally resulting from so unusual a combination as radishes and babies. That is why my balls are rare festivals—the babies will insist on having radishes for the supper, and I, as a decent parent with a proper sense of my responsibilities, am forced accordingly to restrict my invitations to two, at the most three, in a year.

When this last one was over I felt considerably exhausted, and had hardly sufficient strength to receive their thanks with civility. An hour's jig-playing with the thermometer at 90 leaves its marks on the most robust; and when they were in bed, and the supper beginning to do its work, I ordered the carriage and the kettle with a view to seeking repose in the forest, taking the opportunity of

escaping before the Man of Wrath should come
in to dinner. The weather has been very hot for
a long time, but the rain in the morning had had
a wonderful effect on my flowers, and as I drove
away I could not help noticing how charming the
borders in front of the house were looking, with
their white hollyhocks, and white snapdragons, and
fringe of feathery marigolds. This gardener has
already changed the whole aspect of the place, and
I believe I have found the right man at last. He
is very young for a head gardener, but on that
account all the more anxious to please me and
keep his situation ; and it is a great comfort to
have to do with somebody who watches and in-
terprets rightly every expression of one's face
and does not need much talking to. He makes
mistakes sometimes in the men he engages, just
as I used to when I did the engaging, and he had
one poor young man as apprentice who very soon,
like the first of my three meek gardeners, went
mad. His madness was of a harmless nature and
took a literary form ; indeed, that was all they
had against him, that he would write books. He
used to sit in the early morning on my special
seats in the garden, and strictly meditate the thank-
less muse when he ought to have been carting

manure; and he made his fellow-apprentices unspeakably wretched by shouting extracts from
Schiller at them across the intervening gooseberry
bushes. Let me hasten to say that I had never
spoken to him, and should not even have known
what he was like if he had not worn eyeglasses,
so that the Man of Wrath's insinuation that I
affect the sanity of my gardeners is entirely
without justification. The eyeglasses struck me
as so odd on a gardener that I asked who he was,
and was told that he had been studying for the
Bar, but could not pass the examinations, and had
taken up gardening in the hope of getting back
his health and spirits. I thought this a very
sensible plan, and was beginning to feel interested
in him when one day the post brought me a
registered packet containing a manuscript play he
had written called "The Lawyer as Gardener,"
dedicated to me. The Man of Wrath and I were
both in it, the Man of Wrath, however, only in the
list of characters, so that he should not feel hurt,
I suppose, for he never appeared on the scenes at
all. As for me, I was represented as going about
quoting Tolstoi in season and out of season to the
gardeners—a thing I protest I never did. The
young man was sent home to his people, and I

have been asking myself ever since what there is about this place that it should so persistently produce books and lunacy?

On the outskirts of the forest, where shafts of dusty sunlight slanted through the trees, children were picking wortleberries for market as I passed last night, with hands and faces and aprons smudged into one blue stain. I had decided to go to a water-mill belonging to the Man of Wrath which lies far away in a clearing, so far away and so lonely and so quiet that the very spirit of peace seems to brood over it for ever ; and all the way the wortleberry carpet was thick and unbroken. Never were the pines more pungent than after the long heat, and their rosy stems flushed pinker as I passed. Presently I got beyond the region of wortleberry-pickers, the children not caring to wander too far into the forest so late, and I jolted over the roots into the gathering shadows more and more pervaded by that feeling that so refreshes me, the feeling of being absolutely alone.

A very ancient man lives in the mill and takes care of it, for it has long been unused, a deaf old man with a clean, toothless face, and no wife to worry him. He informed me once that all women are mistakes, especially that aggravated form called wives, and that he was thankful he had never married. I felt a certain delicacy after that about intruding on his solitude with the burden of my sex and wifehood heavy upon me, but he always seems very glad to see me, and runs at once to his fowl-house to look for fresh eggs for my tea ; so perhaps he regards me as a pleasing exception to the rule. On this last occasion he brought a table out to the elm tree by the mill stream, that I might get what air there was while I ate my supper ; and I sat in great peace waiting for the kettle to boil and watching the sun dropping behind the sharp forest line, and all the little pools and currents into which the stream just there breaks as it flows over mud banks, ablaze with the red reflection of the sky. The pools are clothed with water-lilies and inhabited by eels, and I generally take a netful of writhing eels back with me to the Man of Wrath to pacify him after my prolonged absence. In the lily time I get into the miller's punt and make them an excuse for paddling about among the mud islands, and even adventurously exploring the river as it winds into the forest, and the old man watches me anxiously from under the elm. He regards my feminine desire to pick water-lilies with indulgence, but is clearly uneasy at my affection for mud banks, and once, after I had stuck on one, and he had run up and down in great agitation for half an hour shouting instructions as to getting off again, he said when I was safely back on shore that people with petticoats (his way of expressing woman) were never intended for punts, and their only chance of safety lay in dry land and keeping quiet. I did not this time attempt the punt, for I was tired, and it was half full of water, probably poured into it by a miller weary of the ways of women; and I drank my tea quietly, going on at the same time with my interrupted afternoon reading of the *Sorrows of Werther*, in which I had reached a part that has a special fascination for me every time I read it—that part where Werther first meets Lotte, and where, after a thunderstorm, they both go to the window, and she is so touched by the beauties of nature that she lays her hand on his and murmurs " Klopstock,"—to the complete dismay of the reader, though not of Werther, for he, we find, was so carried away by the magic word that he flung himself on to her hand and kissed it with tears of rapture.

I looked up from the book at the quiet pools and the black line of trees, above which stars

were beginning to twinkle, my ears soothed by
the splashing of the mill stream and the hooting
somewhere near of a solitary owl, and I wondered
whether, if the Man of Wrath were by my
side, it would be a relief to my pleasurable
feelings to murmur " Klopstock," and whether
if I did he would immediately shed tears of joy
over my hand. The name is an unfortunate
one as far as music goes, and Goethe's putting it
into his heroine's mouth just when she was most
enraptured, seems to support the view I sometimes
adopt in discoursing to the Man of Wrath that he
had no sense of humour. But here I am talking
about Goethe, our great genius and idol, in a way
that no woman should. What do German women
know of such things? Quite untrained and un-
educated, how are we to judge rightly about
anybody or anything? All we can do is to jump
at conclusions, and, when we have jumped, receive
with meekness the information that we have
jumped wrong. Sitting there long after it was
too dark to read, I thought of the old miller's
words, and agreed with him that the best thing a
woman can do in this world is to keep quiet.
He came out once and asked whether he should
bring a lamp, and seemed uneasy at my choosing

to sit there in the dark. I could see the stars in
the black pools, and a line of faint light far away
above the pines where the sun had set. Every
now and then the hot air from the ground struck
up in my face, and afterwards would come a cooler
breath from the water. Of what use is it to fight
for things and make a noise? Nature is so clear
in her teaching that he who has lived with her for
any time can be in little doubt as to the "better
way." Keep quiet and say one's prayers—certainly
not merely the best, but the only things to do if
one would be truly happy ; but, ashamed of asking
when I have received so much, the only form of
prayer I would use would be a form of thanks-
giving.

September

SEPTEMBER

September 9th.—I have been looking in the dictionary for the English word for *Einquartierung*, because that is what is happening to us just now, but I can find nothing satisfactory. My dictionary merely says (1) the quartering, (2) soldiers quartered, and then relapses into irrelevancy ; so that it is obvious English people do without the word for the delightful reason that they have not got the thing. We have it here very badly ; an epidemic raging at the end of nearly every summer, when cottages and farms swarm with soldiers and horses, when all the female part of the population gets engaged to be married and will not work, when all the male part is jealous and wants to fight, and when my house is crowded with individuals so brilliant and decorative in their dazzling uniforms that I wish sometimes I might keep a bunch of the tallest and slenderest for ever in a big china vase in a corner of the drawing-room.

This year the manœuvres are up our way, so that we are blest with more than our usual share of attention, and wherever you go you see soldiers, and the holy calm that has brooded over us all the summer has given place to a perpetual running to and fro of officers' servants, to meals being got ready at all hours, to the clanking of spurs and all those other mysterious things on an officer that do clank whenever he moves, and to the grievous wailings of my unfortunate menials, who are quite beside themselves, and know not whither to turn for succour. We have had one week of it already, and we have yet another before us. There are five hundred men with their horses quartered at the farm, and thirty officers with their servants in our house, besides all those billeted on the surrounding villages who have to be invited to dinner and cannot be allowed to perish in peasant houses ; so that my summer has for a time entirely ceased to be solitary, and whenever I flee distracted to the farthest recesses of my garden and begin to muse, according to my habit, on Man, on Nature, and on Human Life, lieutenants got up in the most exquisite flannels pursue me and want to play tennis with me, a game I have always particularly disliked.

There is no room of course for all those extra men and horses at the farm, and when a few days before their arrival (sometimes it is only one, and sometimes only a few hours) an official appears and informs us of the number to be billeted on us, the Man of Wrath has to have temporary sheds run up, some as stables, some as sleeping-places, and some as dining-rooms. Nor is it easy to cook for five hundred people more than usual, and all the ordinary business of the farm comes to a stand-still while the hands prepare barrowfuls of bacon and potatoes, and stir up the coffee and milk and sugar together with a pole in a tub. Part of the regimental band is here, the upper part. The base instruments are in the next village; but that did not deter an enthusiastic young officer from marching his men past our windows on their arrival at six in the morning, with colours flying, and what he had of his band playing their tunes as unconcernedly as though all those big things that make such a noise were giving the fabric its accustomed and necessary base. We are paid six pfennings a day for lodging a common soldier, and six pfennings for his horse—rather more than a penny in English money for the pair of them; only unfortunately sheds and carpentry are not quite so cheap. Eighty pfennings a day is added for the soldier's food, and for this he has to receive two pounds of bread, half a pound of meat, a quarter of a pound of bacon, and either a quarter of a pound of rice or barley or three pounds of potatoes. Officers are paid for at the rate of two marks fifty a day without wine; we are not obliged to give them wine, and if we do they are regarded as guests, and behave accordingly. The thirty we have now do not, as I could have wished, all go out together in the morning and stay out till the evening, but some go out as others come in, and breakfast is not finished till lunch begins, and lunch drags on till dinner, and all day long the dining-room is full of meals and officers, and we ceased a week ago to have the least feeling that the place, after all, belongs to us.

Now really it seems to me that I am a much-tried woman, and any peace I have enjoyed up to now is amply compensated for by my present torments. I believe even my stern friend the missionary would be satisfied if he could know how swiftly his prediction that sorrow and suffering would be sure to come, has been fulfilled. All day long I am giving out table linen, ordering meals, supporting the feeble knees of servants, making appropriate and amiable remarks to officers, presiding as gracefully as nature permits at meals, and trying to look as though I were happy ; while out in the garden—oh, I know how it is looking out in the garden this golden weather, how the placid hours are slipping by in unchanged peace, how strong the scent of roses and ripe fruit is, how the sleepy bees drone round the flowers, how warmly the sun shines in that corner where the little Spanish chestnut is turning yellow—the first to turn, and never afterwards surpassed in autumn beauty ; I know how still it is down there in my fir wood, where the insects hum undisturbed in the warm, quiet air ; I know what the plain looks like from the seat under the oak, how beautiful, with its rolling green waves burning to gold under the afternoon sky ; I know how the hawks circle over it, and how the larks sing above it, and I edge as near to the open window as I can, straining my ears to hear them, and forgetting the young men who are telling me of all the races their horses win as completely as though they did not exist. I want to be out there

on that golden grass, and look up into that endless
blue, and feel the ecstasy of that song through all
my being, and there is a tearing at my heart when
I remember that I cannot.   Yet they are beautiful
young men ; all are touchingly amiable, and many
of the older ones even charming—how is it, then,
that I so passionately prefer larks ?

We have every grade of greatness here, from
that innocent being the ensign, a creature of
apparent modesty and blushes, who is obliged to
stand up and drain his glass each time a superior
chooses to drink to him, and who sits on the
hardest chairs and looks for the balls while we
play tennis, to the general, invariably delightful,
whose brains have carried him triumphantly
through the annual perils of weeding out, who is
as distinguished in looks and manners as he is in
abilities, and has the crowning merit of being manifestly happy in the society of women.   Nothing
lower than a colonel is to me an object of interest.
The lower you get the more officers there are, and
the harder it is to see the promising ones in the
crowd ; but once past the rank of major the air
gets very much cleared by the merciless way they
have been weeded out, and the higher officers are
the very flower of middle-aged German males.

As for those below, a lieutenant is a bright and beautiful being who admires no one so much as himself; a captain is generally newly married, having reached the stage of increased pay which makes a wife possible, and, being often still in love with her, is ineffective for social purposes; and a major is a man with a yearly-increasing family, for whose wants his pay is inadequate, a person continually haunted by the fear of approaching weeding, after which his career is ended, he is poorer than ever, and being no longer young and only used to a soldier's life, is almost always quite incapable of starting afresh. Even the children of light find it difficult to start afresh with any success after forty, and the retired officer is never a child of light; if he were, he would not have been weeded out. You meet him everywhere, shorn of the glories of his uniform, easily recognisable by the bad fit of his civilian clothes, wandering about like a ship without a rudder; and as time goes on he settles down to the inevitable, and passes his days in a fourth-floor flat in the suburbs, eats, drinks, sleeps, reads the *Kreuzzeitung* and nothing else, plays at cards in the day-time, grows gouty, and worries his wife. It would be difficult to count the number of them that have answered the Man of Wrath's advertisements for book-keepers and secretaries—always vainly, for even if they were fit for the work, no single person possesses enough tact to cope successfully with the peculiarities of such a situation. I hear that some English people of a hopeful disposition indulge in ladies as servants; the cases are parallel, and the tact required to meet both superhuman.

Of all the officers here the only ones with whom I can find plenty to talk about are the generals. On what subject under heaven could one talk to a lieutenant? I cannot discuss the agility of ballet-dancers or the merits of jockeys with him, because these things are as dust and ashes to me ; and when forced for a few moments by my duties as hostess to come within range of his conversation I feel chilly and grown old. In the early spring of this year, in those wonderful days of hope when nature is in a state of suppressed excitement, and when any day the yearly recurring miracle may happen of a few hours' warm rain changing the whole world, we got news that a lieutenant and two men with their horses were imminent, and would be quartered here for three nights while some occult military evolutions were going on a few miles off. It was specially

inopportune, because the Man of Wrath would
not be here, but he comforted me as I bade him
good-bye, my face no doubt very blank, by the
assurance that the lieutenant would be away all
day, and so worn out when he got back in the
evening that he probably would not appear at all.
But I never met a more wide-awake young man.
Not once during those three days did he respond
to my pressing entreaties to go and lie down, and
not all the desperate eloquence of a woman at her
wits' end could persuade him that he was very
tired and ought to try and get some sleep. I had
intended to be out when he arrived, and to remain
out till dinner time, but he came unexpectedly
early, while the babies and I were still at lunch,
the door opening to admit the most beautiful
specimen of his class that I have ever seen, so
beautiful indeed in his white uniform that the
babies took him for an angel-visitant of the type
that visited Abraham and Sarah, and began in
whispers to argue about wings. He was not in
the least tired after his long ride he told me, in
reply to my anxious inquiries, and, rising to the
occasion, at once plunged into conversation, evidently realising how peculiarly awful prolonged
pauses under the circumstances would be. I took

him for a drive in the afternoon, after having
vainly urged him to rest, and while he told me
about his horses, and his regiment, and his brother
officers, in what at last grew to be a decidedly
intermittent prattle, I amused myself by wondering
what he would say if I suddenly began to hold
forth on the themes I love best, and insist that he
should note the beauty of the trees as they stood
that afternoon expectant, with all their little buds
only waiting for the one warm shower to burst
into the glory of young summer.   Perhaps he
would regard me as the German variety of a
hyena in petticoats—the imagination recoils before
the probable fearfulness of such an animal—or, if
not quite so bad as that, at any rate a creature
hysterically inclined ; and he would begin to feel
lonely, and think of his comrades, and his pleasant
mess, and perhaps even of his mother, for he was
very young and newly fledged.   Therefore I held
my peace, and restricted my conversation to things
military, of which I know probably less than any
other woman in Germany, so that my remarks
must have been to an unusual degree impressive.
He talked down to me, and I talked down to him,
and we reached home in a state of profoundest
exhaustion—at least I know I did, but when I

looked at him he had not visibly turned a hair. I went upstairs trying to hope that he had felt it more than he showed, and that during the remainder of his stay he would adopt the suggestion so eagerly offered of spending his spare time in his room resting.

At dinner he and I, quite by ourselves, were both manifestly convinced of the necessity, for the sake of the servants, of not letting the conversation drop. I felt desperate, and would have said anything sooner than sit opposite him in silence, and with united efforts we got through that fairly well. After dinner I tried gossip, and encouraged him to tell me some, but he had such an unnatural number of relations that whoever I began to talk about happened to be his cousin, or his brother-in-law, or his aunt, as he hastily informed me, so that what I had intended to say had to be turned immediately into loud and unqualified praise ; and praising people is frightfully hard work—you give yourself the greatest pains over it, and are aware all the time that it is not in the very least carrying conviction. Does not everybody know that one's natural impulse is to tear the absent limb from limb ? At half-past nine I got up, worn out in mind and body, and told him very firmly that it had been a custom in my family from time immemorial to be in bed by ten, and that I was accordingly going there. He looked surprised and wider awake than ever, but nothing shook me, and I walked away, leaving him standing on the hearthrug after the manner of my countrymen, who never dream of opening a door for a woman.

The next day he went off at five in the morning, and was to be away, as he had told me, till the evening. I felt as though I had been let out of prison as I breakfasted joyfully on the verandah, the sun streaming through the creeperless trellis on to the little meal, and the first cuckoo of the year calling to me from the fir wood. Of the dinner and evening before me I would not think ; indeed I had a half-formed plan in my head of going to the forest after lunch with the babies, taking wraps and provisions, and getting lost till well on towards bedtime ; so that when the angel-visitant should return full of renewed strength and conversation, he would find the casket empty and be told the gem had gone out for a walk. After I had finished breakfast I ran down the steps into the garden, intent on making the most of every minute and hardly able to keep my feet from dancing. Oh, the blessedness of a bright spring morning without a lieutenant! And was there ever such a hopeful beginning to a day, and so full of promise for the subsequent right passing of its hours, as breakfast in the garden, alone with your teapot and your book! Any cobwebs that have clung to your soul from the day before are brushed off with a neatness and expedition altogether surprising; never do tea and toast taste so nice as out there in the sun; never was book so wise and full of pith as the one lying open before you; never was woman so clean outside and in, so refreshed, so morally and physically well-tubbed, as she who can start her day in this fashion. As I danced down the garden path I began to think cheerfully even of lieutenants. It was not so bad; he would be away till dark, and probably on the morrow as well; I would start off in the afternoon, and by coming back very late would not see him at all that day—might not, if Providence were kind, see him again ever; and this last thought was so exhilarating that I began to sing. But he came back just as we had finished lunch.

"The *Herr Lieutenant* is here," announced the servant, "and has gone to wash his hands. The

Herr Lieutenant has not yet lunched, and will be down in a moment."

"I want the carriage at once," I ordered—I could not and would not spend another afternoon *tête-à-tête* with that young man,—"and you are to tell the *Herr Lieutenant* that I am sorry I was obliged to go out, but I had promised the pastor to take the children there this afternoon. See that he has everything he wants."

I gathered the babies together and fled. I could hear the lieutenant throwing things about overhead, and felt there was not a moment to lose. The servant's face showed plainly that he did not believe about the pastor, and the babies looked up at me wonderingly. What is a woman to do when driven into a corner? The father of lies inhabits corners—no doubt the proper place for such a naughty person.

We ran upstairs to get ready. There was only one short flight on which we could meet the lieutenant, and once past that we were safe; but we met him on that one short flight. He was coming down in a hurry, giving his moustache a final hasty twist, and looking fresher, brighter, lovelier, than ever.

"Oh, good morning. You have got back

much sooner than you expected, have you not?"
I said lamely.

"Yes, I managed to get through my part
quickly," he said with a briskness I did not like.

"But you started so early—you must be very
tired?"

"Oh, not in the least, thank you."

Then I repeated the story about the expectant
parson, adding to my guilt by laying stress on the
inevitability of the expedition owing to its having
been planned weeks before. April and May stood
on the landing above, listening with surprised
faces, and June, her mind evidently dwelling on
feathers, intently examined his shoulders from the
step immediately behind. And we did get away,
leaving him to think what he liked, and to smoke,
or sleep, or wander as he chose, and I could not
but believe he must feel relieved to be rid of me ;
but the afternoon clouded over, and a sharp wind
sprang up, and we were very cold in the forest,
and the babies began to sneeze and ask where the
parson was, and at last, after driving many miles,
I said it was too late to go to the parson's and we
would turn back. It struck me as hard that we
should be forced to wander in cold forests and
leave our comfortable home because of a lieutenant,

and I went back with my heart hardened against him.

That second evening was worse a great deal than the first. We had said all we ever meant to say to each other, and had lauded all our relations with such hearty goodwill that there was nothing whatever to add. I sat listening to the slow ticking of the clock and asking questions about things I did not in the least want to know, such as the daily work and rations and pay of the soldiers in his regiment, and presently—we having dined at the early hour usual in the country—the clock struck eight. Could I go to bed at eight? No, I had not the courage, and no excuse ready. More slow ticking, and more questions and answers about rations and pipeclay. What a clock! For utter laziness and dull deliberation there surely never was its equal—it took longer to get to the half-hour than any clock I ever met, but it did get there at last and struck it. Could I go? Could I? No, still no excuse ready. We drifted from pipeclay to a discussion on bicycling for women—a dreary subject. Was it becoming? Was it good for them? Was it ladylike? Ought they to wear skirts or ——? In Paris they all wore ——. Our bringing-up here is so excellent that if we tried we could not induce ourselves to speak of any forked garments to a young man, so we make ourselves understood, when we desire to insinuate such things, by an expressive pause and a modest downward flicker of the eyelids. The clock struck nine. Nothing should keep me longer. I sprang to my feet and said I was exhausted beyond measure by the sharp air driving, and that whenever I had spent an afternoon out, it was my habit to go to bed half an hour earlier than other evenings. Again he looked surprised, but rather less so than the night before, and he was, I think, beginning to get used to me. I retired, firmly determined not to face another such day and to be very ill in the morning and quite unable to rise, he having casually remarked that the next one was an off day ; and I would remain in bed, that last refuge of the wretched, as long as he remained here.

I sat by the window in my room till late, looking out at the moonlight in the quiet garden, with a feeling as though I were stuffed with sawdust — a very awful feeling — and thinking ruefully of the day that had begun so brightly and ended so dismally. What a miserable thing not to be able to be frank and say simply,

" My good young man, you and I never saw each other before, probably won't see each other again, and have no interests in common. I mean you to be comfortable in my house, but I want to be comfortable too. Let us, therefore, keep out of each other's way while you are obliged to be here. Do as you like, go where you like, and order what you like, but don't expect me to waste my time sitting by your side and making small-talk. I too have to get to heaven, and have no time to lose. You won't see me again. Good-bye."

I believe many a harassed *Hausfrau* would give much to be able to make some such speech when these young men appear, and surely the young men themselves would be grateful ; but simplicity is apparently quite beyond people's strength. It is, of all the virtues, the one I prize the most ; it is undoubtedly the most lovable of any, and unspeakably precious for its power of removing those mountains that confine our lives and prevent our seeing the sky. Certain it is that until we have it, the simple spirit of the little child, we shall in no wise discover our kingdom of heaven.

These were my reflections, and many others

besides, as I sat weary at the window that cold spring night, long after the lieutenant who had occasioned them was slumbering peacefully on the other side of the house. Thoughts of the next day, and enforced bed, and the bowls of gruel to be disposed of if the servants were to believe in my illness, made my head ache. Eating gruel *pour la galérie* is a pitiable state to be reduced to — surely no lower depths of humiliation are conceivable. And then, just as I was drearily remembering how little I loved gruel, there was a sudden sound of wheels rolling swiftly round the corner of the house, a great rattling and trampling in the still night over the stones, and tearing open the window and leaning out, there, sitting in a station fly, and apparelled to my glad vision in celestial light, I beheld the Man of Wrath, come home unexpectedly to save me.

"Oh, dear Man of Wrath," I cried, hanging out into the moonlight with outstretched arms, "how much nicer thou art than lieutenants! I never missed thee more — I never longed for thee more — I never loved thee more — come up here quickly that I may kiss thee!"

October 1st.—Last night after dinner, when we were in the library, I said, "Now listen to me, Man of Wrath."

"Well?" he inquired, looking up at me from the depths of his chair as I stood before him.

"Do you know that as a prophet you are a failure? Five months ago to-day you sat among the wallflowers and scoffed at the idea of my being able to enjoy myself alone a whole summer through. Is the summer over?"

"It is," he assented, as he heard the rain beating against the windows.

"And have I invited any one here?"

"No, but there were all those officers."

"They have nothing whatever to do with it."

"They helped you through one fortnight."

"They didn't. It was a fortnight of horror."

"Well. Go on."

"You said I would be punished by being dull. Have I been dull?"

"My dear, as though if you had been you would ever confess it."

"That's true. But as a matter of fact let me tell you that I never spent a happier summer."

He merely looked at me out of the corners of his eyes.

" If I remember rightly," he said, after a pause, " your chief reason for wishing to be solitary was that your soul might have time to grow. May I ask if it did ? "

" Not a bit."

He laughed, and, getting up, came and stood by my side before the fire. "At least you are honest," he said, drawing my hand through his arm.

" It is an estimable virtue."

" And strangely rare in woman."

" Now leave woman alone. I have discovered you know nothing really of her at all. But *I* know all about her."

" You do ? My dear, one woman can never judge the others."

" An exploded tradition, dear Sage."

" Her opinions are necessarily biassed."

" Venerable nonsense, dear Sage."

" Because women are each other's natural enemies."

" Obsolete jargon, dear Sage."

" Well, what do you make of her ? "

" Why, that she's a DEAR, and that you ought to be very happy and thankful to have got one of her always with you."

" But am I not ? " he asked, putting his arm

round me and looking affectionate ; and when people begin to look affectionate I, for one, cease to take any further interest in them.

And so the Man of Wrath and I fade away into dimness and muteness, my head resting on his shoulder, and his arm encircling my waist ; and what could possibly be more proper, more praise-worthy, or more picturesque ?

THE END

VIRAGO MODERN CLASSICS

The first Virago Modern Classic, *Frost in May* by Antonia White, was published in 1978. It launched a list dedicated to the celebration of women writers and to the rediscovery and reprinting of their works. Its aim was, and is, to demonstrate the existence of a female tradition in fiction which is both enriching and enjoyable, and to broaden the sometimes narrow academic definition of a 'classic' which has often led to the neglect of a large number of interesting secondary works of fiction. In calling the series 'Modern Classics' we do not necessarily mean 'great' — although this is often the case. Published with new critical and biographical introductions, books are chosen for many reasons: sometimes for their importance in literary history; sometimes because they illuminate particular aspects of women's lives, both personal and public. They may be classics of comedy or storytelling; their interest can be historical, feminist, political or literary.

Initially the Virago Modern Classics concentrated on English novels and short stories published in the early decades of this century. As the series has grown it has broadened to include works of fiction from different centuries, different countries, cultures and literary traditions, many of which have been suggested by our readers.